THE
CIRCLE AND
THE EQUATOR

THE
CIRCLE AND
THE EQUATOR
KYRA GIORGI

UWA PUBLISHING

First published in 2017 by
UWA Publishing
Crawley, Western Australia 6009
www.uwap.uwa.edu.au

UWAP is an imprint of UWA Publishing,
a division of The University of Western Australia.

THE UNIVERSITY OF
WESTERN
AUSTRALIA

Two of the stories in this collection have been published before, in earlier drafts:
'The Circle and the Equator' in *Overland* 217, 2014.
'Moon Tide', as 'Burn-in' in *The Irish Times*, 2014.

National Library of Australia Cataloguing-in-Publication data:

Giorgi, Kyra, author.
The circle and the equator / Kyra Giorgi.
ISBN: 9781742589237 (paperback)
Short stories.

Typeset in Bembo by Lasertype
Cover design by Alissa Dinallo
Cover image: *Rainbow Mask*, Lajos Vajda, 1938, pastel on paper.
Image courtesy of Wikimedia Commons.
Printed by Lightning Source

This project has been assisted by the Copyright Agency Cultural Fund

for my mum

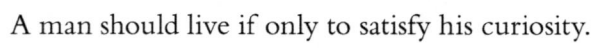
A man should live if only to satisfy his curiosity.

– Yiddish proverb

Contents

1

The circle and the equator

Cassinga, Angola, 1978

I

The first time I saw Tercero I didn't know what I was seeing. His head loomed over me, and I thought he must be a spirit or an animal, or a combination of the two. From his mouth came a language that rolled and bubbled and spat like boiling water. It was awful. I had never seen a white person before and now here was one with his green eyes fixed on me and his meaty arms around me, scooping me, jostling me along. I cried for my mother, but she did not come. And then from the white face came a different sound, a *schhhhsh*, *schhhhsh*, that recalled wind caressing sand, and my eyes would not stay open any more.

What I remember – what I know – has been delivered to me by the other children who were there that day. It was early and the sun had begun its gentle blaze through the treetops. As on every other morning we were gathered outside, along with our parents and the soldiers, to salute our flag. It fluttered against the pearly sky from which, seconds later, a succession of white pellets fell. At the same moment we heard a plane overhead. What I do recall, all by myself, is that there was a great excitement among us children, because somebody shouted that the pellets were sweets, and the plane was the President's plane, and he was dropping them for us, a special treat. We were refugees – the idea that sweets could fall from the sky was unthinkable, but then thinking was a luxury, too. Our feet shuffled on the dusty ground as we became ever more excited, while our horrified guardians realised what was going on. Then the first bomb hit the ground and our joy shattered, irretrievable in the general panic. I was pulled up very hard by one arm, I suppose by my mother, and at some point the tension dropped off and I was alone, and the bombs continued to fall, shaking the air, shaking us – and there I stopped gathering memories for a while. After that the paratroopers came, and then the Cubans to chase them out, but I missed all of that. That was why the first white face I saw was Tercero's.

The South African government forces had followed us to our haven. We Namibians had fled into Angola and were living in Cassinga, in a camp run by the armed wing of the SWAPO, our party of national liberation. There were quite a few of us, and of those like me – children with a mother or father, but not both. I think I had been a refugee since I was born. I had no sense of home, or of any place to return to. There was only forward.

For a long time I was glad that I had not seen the body of my mother, as some children had, decomposing in a pile with others in a hollow in the ground. But later I wished I could have seen something of her – even if it wasn't really her, but just a glimpse of her hair or a fragment of her dress, the one with the bird pattern that she was wearing that day. I think they buried her before I woke up. In any case, I didn't see her again.

Many years later, Tercero told me that the raid on our camp might actually have saved my life. I'd had malaria, and was malnourished, anaemic – I might not have received proper treatment otherwise. He was a medic who had arrived with the Cuban soldiers to save us. They had a base not far from Cassinga, and when news of the attack broke, they rushed to our aid, but too late, he said, to save all of us. Hundreds perished. I should count myself lucky, he said.

The refrain followed us thereafter. We were lucky. We had survived the imperialist attack. We were the hope of a new, internationalist Africa. We embodied socialist ideals and the promise of youth. Cuba would help us break the shackles of apartheid and we would return, victorious, to an independent Namibia. When we moved from Cassinga to another camp in the north, we were taught it all again, but in Spanish this time. As we sat repeating our *yo soy*, *tú eres*, we could hear the thump of earth as the soldiers dug trenches around us, just in case our new camp should also come under attack.

2

Before he left, Tercero taught me two very important things. First, that if I felt lonely I should think of him, because he would forever be my friend in the world. Second, how to remove my shrapnel. Fragments of the bomb that had knocked me out had also embedded

3

themselves in my face and body, and the blast had sent other broken bits of the camp flying into me too. A shard of metal became lodged in my side, and another entered my shoulder, but these larger pieces were surgically removed after the raid. Then I healed. The wounds closed over, my body remade its armour. But one day, while idly picking at my scars, I noticed that certain places felt hard, like there was a grain of rice under the skin. Some of them hurt when I pressed them, and so I pressed them some more, half in irritation and half in curiosity.

'Leave them alone,' Tercero advised, 'and they'll come out on their own.' They were the minute fragments the Cuban doctors had left inside me. 'But I wouldn't worry. Your body doesn't like the taste of metal, so it spits it out eventually.' Tercero told me that when I could feel or see a fragment emerging I should ask a nurse for help, but he didn't seem to believe I would, because he showed me how to use my fingernails to prise out the foreign bodies, and even gave me a small glass jar to put them in. 'Next time I see you you'll have a fine collection!' he said.

When the first piece began to emerge – a tiny disc of metal from my left thigh – I sat down on the ground and, positioning the nails of my thumbs just as I had been instructed, carefully lifted it out. It slid to the surface without a sound or protest, like a ripe berry that detaches from its stalk at the slightest touch. I examined it on my fingertip. Such a tiny thing! I wondered how many smithereens that bomb had blown, and how many it had blown into me. I spat on the wound, which had begun to bleed a little, and, as I anticipated the next addition to my new collection, was filled with a sense of achievement.

I was not the only child with shrapnel wounds. If we waited long enough our fragments might push themselves all the way out, but they were itchy and irritating, and it was impossible for us not to pick at the little shards as they began to emerge. One boy, who insisted on being called by his newly adopted name, Artúlio, was particularly taken with my collection, a modest confetti of metal, glass and plastic. We both coveted especially a green plastic piece, a lovely, still-vivid emerald, that we guessed had come from a bucket that had been sitting in the courtyard. Massaging the bumps under our skin, we played guessing games, trying to predict what our bodies would reveal next.

At the end of the year they took us to Cuba, as promised. From Luanda to Havana, and then under a heavy indigo sky towards a small town on the coast, where I smelled and tasted the sea for the first time. There the sky broke as we knew it would, for it had mirrored our exhaustion. And while the heavens were still flecked with rain, we continued our journey, now across the slapping ocean, to a place proclaimed the Island of Youth. In that name was the promise not of youth but arrest – after a lifetime of moving, the declaration that we would live, study and work on the island until we were adults seemed like the story of the rest of our lives.

3

Every morning revolution infiltrated our dreams. From huge loudspeakers, radio broadcasts informing us of quotas exceeded or enemies trounced crackled through our sleepy heads. Our dormitory was for Namibian children only; others housed children from more distant parts of Africa and the world. For half the day we learnt about our people's campaign for independence, the Cuban Revolution, mathematics and the socialist struggle against imperialism. For the other we worked in the fields, harvesting lemons, oranges and grapefruit. We took turns to attend to the chickens and goats, and the vegetables we would later eat. It was not always easy, but we were self-sufficient and building a bright future for ourselves and for the world.

My injuries did not prevent me from working hard; I was able to do as much as anyone else. I still collected fragments from my body, but after a few years the seam ran dry. That was a relief. The exit of the fragments, not always at the point from which they had entered, created new scars, and my face and neck were furrowed with grooves and ridges. Now the pleasant anticipation of expanding my collection had gone, I became newly aware of the disfigurement the bomb had caused. I compared my riddled skin to that of the other children, the ones whose bodies had not been thrown about by the wind of a blast. They were refugees too, but their stories were not written on them so clearly as mine. Yet it was not done to dwell on this. There was the implicit understanding that we Cassinga children were special. And in this, exceptional behaviour and forbearance were expected of us.

By lights out, the memory of our cacophonous awakening had dissipated into the silence of the dormitory. Into that space crept our families – the dead and distant and disappeared – and we sang to them with our sobs and prayers. I wanted to be stronger, but the night had such vastness, such depth...It was the space for a sorrow so pure that I could not resist plunging into it with the rest. That was what the night was there for, after all. To submerge and suffocate us, to wring from us every last drop of memory and consciousness, so that finally we could sleep.

4

Every year, on the occasion of 1 May, the *Dia del Trabajo*, a card would arrive from Tercero addressed to us all. Then one day they stopped. The last arrived when I was eleven. It had been brief, a perfunctory message of good wishes that I should have known foretold his detachment from us. The following year I waited until August before I conceded that no card was coming, but I did not give up. I decided to write to him instead. As a model student I was eventually permitted to send a letter to our doctor, our saviour.

Dear Comrade Doctor Tercero Martins,

How are you? Well, I hope. I am sorry to inform you that we did not receive your card this year, so that is why I am writing to you. What is it like in Havana? Do you work in the hospital there? They say it is very nice. I have been to our capital, but it was only for a few hours so I don't remember much. I didn't see the Castle or the Plaza Vieja or anything like that. I hope that one day I will go to university in Havana. I want to study medicine and be a doctor too. I am studying very hard and my teachers say I will be one for sure. Maybe in Cuba or maybe in Namibia. For now, I don't know. Our nation is not free yet but it is only a matter of time because the struggle continues.

We are all very happy here and everybody says hello.
We are wishing you and your family a happy Dia del
Trabajo, even if it is a little bit late, and we hope you will
write to us again and not forget us.
    ¡Hasta la victoria siempre!
    Yours sincerely,
    Helvi Maria

These were not exactly my words – I'd had to rewrite the letter a bit for approval, and they'd made me collect signatures from the other students as well. I wasn't pleased with this, as I had wanted the letter to be just from me. For a year, perhaps more, Tercero had been by my side – he had nursed my wounds, tucked me in at night, played games with me – and while he had done the same with the others I had been sure that I was his favourite. Each morning for months, though the revolutionary broadcasts clamoured for our undivided attention, my waking thought was whether I would receive a reply that day. Then one morning there was a shift, and a different thought replaced it, the remnants of a dream I had been having when the broadcast began, something unresolved, which felt in that moment more urgent than anything else. Time seemed to be composed of semi-transparent layers that drifted down in between hopes and memories, separating them out, distancing them from me.

And yet I could not imagine that Tercero would not turn up again some day, just to check up on me, to make sure I was studying hard, to give me advice, and observe how I would turn out to be a doctor like him. Subconsciously, I prepared myself for the event, telling my teachers, to all-round approval, of my ambitions. I read books on biology and nature. I devoured entries about phagocytosis, memorised the parts of the brain and their functions, and carried out, with scientific rigour, the mechanisms of crying. I learnt that we are born with more bones than we die with, that the brain is as soft as a banana, and that the skin has many layers. I tried to imagine what had happened to my skin when those fragments of the world penetrated it, then made their way up through the dermis and epithelium – what they broke through, and what they left intact. Now there was nothing left but scar tissue, and something invisible beneath the surface, like roots. By expelling the fragments my body had been protecting me, knitting me back together to prepare me for the years ahead.

5

They looked after us, our hosts did; they made sure our youth was developing in the correct way, along the right path, towards the proper destiny. Every so often we underwent a general medical, which I always passed: my weight was healthy, my teeth were good, I rarely fell ill and was strong, and my scars looked better and better. That year when I was called for my check-up I positively bounded forward – this was my favourite kind of test, one I did not have to study for to pass.

The nurse was new, not one I'd had before. Like most of the school staff she was Cuban, but she was also exceptionally fair – even her eyelashes were pale, almost white – and along with the dusting of freckles they looked like things that had been dried and carried by the wind, like hay or pollen, to settle on her face.

'Ah, a Cassinga baby...' she said, leafing through my file. She read further in silence, betraying no judgement on my illustrious past. 'Good. Now, let's have a look at you.'

There followed a sequence of poking, pressing, weighing and measuring, punctuated by the odd instructional murmur. Then the questioning: did I feel well, when was I last sick, was I checking my shrapnel regularly.

'I don't have any shrapnel,' I said. 'It all came out.'

'Did it now. And when did it all come out?'

'The last one was two and a half years ago, here.' I showed her a small scar on my shoulder.

'Hmm.' She looked at the notes again and began to gently palpate the area between my neck and right shoulder. 'Can you feel that?' I shook my head. 'You've got a big scar there, and I think I can feel a fragment underneath it.'

I told her that all the large fragments had been removed in surgery, after the blast.

'Sometimes,' she said, making her way back round to face me, 'doctors don't remove all the big pieces. Sometimes it's too difficult, and they decide it's better to leave them in there rather than take them out. Did nobody explain that to you?'

'No.'

'Well, perhaps that's because you were very young. But now you can understand. You might still have some fragments in you, and you should be checking them. That's because sometimes shrapnel doesn't want to come out; it gets confused and goes in the wrong direction. So we have to keep an eye on them to make sure they don't decide to migrate where they shouldn't. Do you understand?'

I didn't understand. How there could still be something inside me. I didn't understand.

'You mustn't worry. I can feel the one here and it's still below the place where it went in, so I think that one's decided to stay put. But I want you to feel it, here...' – she guided my hand to the place and she was right, there was something there, beneath the ridges of the scar – '...and remember where it is. We don't want it deciding to go on a journey to your neck, do we?'

The fair-skinned nurse found one more spot where she thought some shrapnel might still be lodged, beneath a scar on my right hip bone. She would check them again next year, but in the meantime I should not prod and poke at these places too much, in case I damaged the surrounding tissue or, worse, prompted them to start a journey. 'But don't worry,' she repeated, 'I expect your fragments are perfectly happy just sitting there and your body has made friends with them. You're a very healthy young woman and very lucky, too.'

As I left and the next child moved forward, I could hear the wind howling outside, a storm coming in over the sea, and I was consumed by a sense of utter failure.

6

This new information did not suit me at all. It did not suit the person I had become. It threatened my sense of possibility; it made my past into a tightening noose. Since I had been told not to provoke my shrapnel, I did.

Why shouldn't I? It had provoked me first! I pinched and prodded and rubbed the troubled sites, urging the pieces to go on their way. They did not belong there – they were intruders. If my body had befriended them then it had done so against my wishes, and they could all go to hell.

Indignation, I discovered then, was a very satisfying emotion. I had never felt it before. Although for years we had been coached to be outraged by the injustices of capitalism, the exploitation of the workers and the arrogance of the Yankee imperialists, I had always been aware of my limitations – never entirely convinced that the emotions I was summoning up were substantially inflamed. But it was just that I had been doing it all wrong; my efforts had not been truthful. Finally I had found my enemy, and my soul trembled and shimmered with a glorious fury.

In the beginning it took me far. It was a useful indigna-tion, easily transferable into the right kind of outrage. In meetings and debates I was always one of the most ardent. Passing my ideological tests was a piece of cake. I exceeded expectations. And all the time I was running alongside a fate that I could not allow to overtake me.

I did not receive a reply from Tercero, but I had long given up waiting for one. I continued my studies as diligently as ever, but without the same enthusiasm. Those passions that were larger and more abstract were much easier to deal with.

My anger swept me through the years and then, in my fifteenth, began to splutter and die. I had moved into *preuniversitario*, and left my nationality group behind. Now I was mixed with the others: Cubans, Angolans and

Mozambicans, Mongolians and North Koreans. At the annual cultural festival we divided up again to present our songs and dances, food and oral traditions, and then came together once more, a kaleidoscopic folding. It was wonderful. I could not remember our traditions, but some of the other Namibians did, and we often joined up with the Angolans, in whose country so many of us had sheltered for so long. I found a boyfriend – a lithe, long-limbed, long-lashed Angolan – who spoke softly and was not a bit interested in my scars, preferring to dwell instead on the smooth skin inside my thighs. When he slid into me, I did not cut him to pieces. The shrapnel had not killed me, nor, as far as I could tell, had it moved at all. In this new world, it had lost its meaning. We had all left something behind; we all carried something with us. I was no different from anybody else.

I never saw Tercero again. When I went to Havana for my medical degree, I often imagined I would bump into him in the street. When I won a scholarship to specialise in surgery, and worked at the general hospital, I kept expecting to see him there – haunting the corridors, looking for somebody to help. But he was not. Perhaps he was practising private medicine, or was away visiting relatives, or had started a new life somewhere. Perhaps he had fallen out of the world and into the Caribbean Sea. Whether the memories he held on to would drag him down or buoy him up, I did not know. I hoped I was one of them. I hoped that I could carry him back to dry land.

2

Soft ground

Berlin, Germany, 1921

That he should find himself wearing the same shoes and —
if it is not too much to believe — the same socks he had
worn a decade ago, that is, before the world was turned
upside down, was an absurdity not lost on Helmut Klück.
His shoes were leather, the colour of a deer, and had been
sitting in a box in his mother's house in a small town
outside Hamburg ever since he'd been called up for service.
His mother had kept them polished in his absence, and she
went on polishing them even after his return, so that now
they had a slightly glistening patina, as if that deer had
been caught in a light rain. They looked especially fine in
this dim, pink-gold afternoon light that seeped graciously
into the train as it vaulted over the iron archways of the
city. Yet age had not softened them; in fact, they were a
great deal stiffer than Helmut remembered. Putting those
shoes on now was like being given regulation-issue boots
all over again: weeks of scraped flesh, blisters and binding
would inevitably follow, but so would that sense of duty,

and the understanding that a little suffering was a natural part of the service of good. One must have faith that sacrifices borne would pay off in the end; one must have faith, because what was there otherwise? His shoes were beautiful, and that was what Sabine would see, and that was all that mattered.

The socks, however, he ought to have thrown away. For all his mother's darning they had not weathered the years well, and he felt undermined by their scruffiness. But if he took care to sit in the right way, not crossing one leg over the other (and so exposing a pre-war sock), Sabine wouldn't notice. So he sat on that train with his knees neatly pursed before him, and his two shiny, beautiful shoes planted flat on the rumbling floor, and he felt almost pleased with himself.

He hoped she would forgive him for not coming sooner. She had left for Berlin at the beginning of the war, perhaps not wanting to wait it out at home with his mother, for the two had never got on very well. She'd sent him her new address, that of her aunt's in Steglitz, but that had been the first and last correspondence from her, and he did not know if the letters he'd sent had ever arrived. Yet he supposed she must still be there, or at the very least that her aunt would be able to tell him where she'd gone. It was true, he ought to have paid a visit sooner, but his long recuperation, the entreaties of his mother, his utter lack of finances and the dark place he'd crawled into in his head... he'd had nothing to present to Sabine that would recall his former self. But eventually he'd emerged again into the world and these past few years had been working to restore himself. Once that was done, not wanting to hurry things, he'd waited another few months – purely out of caution – just long enough to become convinced that the self he had rebuilt was not a cipher, but a man who could withstand all the elements of a normal life. Of course his mother had cautioned him against going. Sabine would be married by now, she said, she'd probably have kids too, and he did have to concede that these were possibilities. An abandoned woman is capable of anything. Somehow, though, it did not trouble him, perhaps because he didn't really think such things possible. His singular belief was that Sabine had only to see him again, and everything would fall back into place.

Perhaps they would live here in the city, if that was what she wanted. She might have become attached to the place – it certainly was different to home – and he had to admit that the distance from his mother might not be a bad thing. He had a vocation now; he could move out and start his life again whenever and wherever he wished. Oh, what a fine future they would have together! The more he thought about it, the more comfortingly logical the idea became.

But this place she had brought herself to! Just look at these people around him. Women, some of them well past their prime, with short boyish hair and thick make-up (he was sure that Sabine had not succumbed to this fashion). And the men, he observed, who came in three broad types: the youngest had the energy and swagger of a generation who had only skirted the edge of war, like those who can enjoy the heady whiff of gasoline without ever having to worry that they might be doused in it; the older ones looked merely tired, and appeared either faintly hostile or improbably jovial, both of which aspects he ascribed to alcohol, although it might also have been that mania of late winter, when the cold is so prolonged and the trees so relentlessly bare that one begins to lose hope it will ever end, and the promise of spring, though dutifully fulfilled each year before, and which is yet present in the blooms of mistletoe nestling in the skeleton trees, still recedes by the day...Under such conditions you cannot blame a man for a little craziness. Nor a woman, for that matter.

And then the third type of man, the one who has departed from the world and then returned. The Ghost. The city was full of them, hollowed and scarred, limping and gazing. There had been one in the carriage with him earlier, and by the time he got off there would no doubt be another. Thankfully, Helmut did not limp, and his face was relatively free from the telltale pockmarks of the gas fields. His persistent cough, on the other hand, might be a bit of a giveaway, but he fancied it could be taken for seasonal sniffles. Thank God for winter! It might drive men mad, but it had its purpose.

At the next stop the train again performed its heart-like emptying and filling. Adjusting their scarves and pulling their coats tight, passengers stepped out into the flurry of snow – a leap of faith – and others stepped in, bringing the slush of the platform with them. A few seats away from him an elderly woman, scarlet in matching lipstick, hat and nose, had just been replaced by a lean young fellow whom Helmut identified immediately as fitting into that first category of man. *Not a worry in the world!* he chuckled to himself, surprisingly devoid of envy, and returned to his thoughts of Sabine and how happy she would be to receive him in less than a couple of hours from now. After a while of minding his own business, however, he noticed that the young man was studying him very intently. He had a kind of folio propped up on one of his knees and was glancing furtively between Helmut and his page, upon which his hand worked in a rapid flicking motion.

My God, is he drawing me?

The young man was certainly brazen. When Helmut caught his eye, with the intention of throwing him an intimidating stare, the stranger shot back a friendly smile. *What* is *he doing?* Helmut thought, increasingly irritated and self-conscious. *Why is he picking on me? At the very least he could ask my permission…*

And then, as if summoned by that thought, the young man rose from his seat and came forward to plant himself firmly upon the empty one opposite Helmut.

'Good afternoon,' he said, holding out a hand. 'I see you caught me in the middle of a little sketch. I hope you don't mind. It's just, you have *such* an interesting face, really, very characterful!'

Not knowing what else to do, Helmut tentatively shook his hand.

'Allow me to introduce myself,' the young man went on, 'Georg Vasilsky, Artist.'

'I am Herr Klück,' Helmut said. Then, as if the name of the six generations before him was suddenly insufficient, added, '*Visitor.*'

'Well, that's a title to shout about! Visitor from where? No, don't tell me, I like the mystery of it. Sometimes the less I know about my subjects the better.'

He was remarkably poised, this artist, warm and firm in his approach but not too loud or overly intimate – as the kind of strangers who approach others on trains often are. His eyes were deep brown and he had a small neat moustache a shade lighter. He wore no hat over his slicked-over head, but was instead festooned in a huge scarf that crowded manfully around his shoulders. His coat was tweed and suited him very well; his shoes were an unusual crimson, with clean black soles. Helmut had the impression that this get-up would have cost a fair bit more than an artist drawing people on trains could afford. But then what did he know of such things – of clothes or, indeed, of art?

'So you were drawing me...' Helmut muttered in semi-inquiry.

'I certainly was, my good fellow.'

'Can I see?'

'Well,' the artist said, 'the thing is it's not finished just yet. Tell you what, though. You can see it when it's done – you just have to let me put on a few finishing touches.'

'I'm getting off in a few stops,' Helmut said.

'Oh, where are you headed?' The artist asked, with a languor that ignored the implied haste. 'You're a visitor, so there must be some lucky one being visited!'

To this Helmut thought it best not to reply.

'And,' the young man leaned forward, 'I bet it's a woman!'

'Well, I – what makes you say that?'

'Forgive me if this sounds impertinent, but I couldn't help noticing that you do seem a bit nervous. Fidgeting with your tie and so forth. I thought then, "Now that's a man on his way to see a lady!" By the same account, I think that's why I began drawing you in the first place. Strong emotions – love – they give our faces something, don't you think?'

'I don't know,' Helmut replied, 'I haven't considered it really.' He was unnerved that he had given away so much simply by sitting there. What would Sabine, who once knew him so well, be able to see in him? Things that even he didn't know were there?

The artist leaned back and took out a hipflask, unscrewed the lid and offered it to Helmut. 'In any case, you look like a man who could use a drink.'

Helmut thanked him and took a sip and then, because he really was very grateful for it, thanked him again. Cognac, not a bad one either. God, how he'd needed that!

'Listen,' the fellow continued, 'you're not in a hurry, I hope? You see there's a wonderful little bar just off Ebersstraße. A real treasure, tucked away, only locals know about it. I'd very much like to finish my picture; I can see this one has real potential...so why don't we get off and let me buy you a drink? I'll make the finishing touches and then you can go on your way. Goodness, that's the next stop! I got all caught up in chatting with you, that's how it is when you meet someone interesting. My point is, just a drink, just to take the edge off – it won't take long. In your shoes I'd need some extra courage! And you know, you'd really be doing me a favour.' Here the young man laid his hand across his heart, stood, tucked his sketchbook away, and bowed lightly to him. 'It would be an honour, but, of course, if you're really in a terrible hurry...'

'No, I mean, not really,' Helmut muttered. He could use a proper drink, and another half-hour wouldn't really make a difference. Sabine wasn't expecting him, after all. Payment for his portrait. Fair enough.

At the next stop they both got off, and Helmut trotted beside his new acquaintance into the speckled dusk. The artist put his hand on his back, ever so slightly urging him forward. 'You can tell me about your time in the war, too, if you like. One thing I've learnt, you soldiers always have such stories to tell!'

So, Helmut thought, dismayed, *he knows. That I am not in the first category of men.* For all his efforts, he had not been able to conceal that.

The bar was indeed not far from the station. It was one of those dim, somewhat cramped caverns that announce themselves from several yards away with the smoke leaking from it. Helmut hesitated; Sabine didn't like the smell of tobacco – she was rather delicate, and had always complained when he'd taken out his pipe in her presence. But he was freezing, his pinched feet were urging him to sit down again, and the artist was ushering him in. Well, he thought, he would still have the distance from the station to her aunt's house – he could walk the smell off in the night air then. And he wouldn't be here long, in any case.

The artist was in a phenomenally good mood, one that seemed to anticipate the festive spirit of the bar, for when he walked in he seemed to be absorbed naturally into it, like a raindrop in a lake. Whereas Helmut was rather a blob of oil on its surface. In the lively atmosphere, though, nobody seemed to notice. The artist claimed a segment of bench and ordered them both a beer and a schnapps.

'Oh, just the beer,' Helmut protested, but all too feebly, as only a pedant would argue that a beer and a schnapps were two separate drinks, so well did they go together, and, after all, he was there to relax.

The alcohol – in retrospect not unpredictably – went straight to his head. He was a slight man, and had not eaten for several hours, not since he woke up that morning in his mother's house. A full breakfast had awaited him: moist, freshly baked rye, fried herrings, picked onions, boiled eggs and cheese. It all seemed very distant now: the still of the dark morning, the smells of bread and milk and clean bedding, and of things pressed and preserved and inured against time. And now here he was, in a bar halfway across the country, a stranger among strangers, having willingly thrown himself into the thick of humanity again. All this noise and life…he didn't know yet if it agreed with him. He had only done it for Sabine. Suddenly he remembered the rolls his mother had prepared him for the journey and that he had forgotten to eat, most likely crushed in their wax paper at the bottom of his bag. He'd had butterflies in his stomach all day. Well, now he would drown those butterflies that had been bothering him so much. Serves them right!

The young artist was happily chatting away about this and that, and Helmut was only half-listening. One of the faculties he'd developed during the war was the ability to concentrate his thoughts into a body of liquid: a glass of beer, a cup of tea, a tub of water, a puddle in a trench – even a patch of melting snow. It was, he was sure, what had preserved his sanity. Thank God he wasn't a Bedouin, living out in a tent somewhere, not a drop of water for miles!

Sipping his beer slowly seemed to help sustain that magical quality in it. Yet it didn't help the tickle in his throat that the smoke was aggravating. He brought the mug of beer up to his mouth and took a modest gulp, but as he was doing so a giant spasm of a cough engulfed him, and he knocked the glass violently against his teeth, propelling most of its contents across the benchtop.

A hand clamped over Helmut's shoulder as he embarked on the bumpy journey that is a coughing fit. 'There, there,' the artist said. 'Never mind, old chap. I'll get you another. Another *Schnäpschen*, too.'

By the time he returned Helmut was still coughing. Tears streaming down his face, his whole body trembling, he dared not pick up the mug with his hands, so instead he lowered his face towards it, his lips meeting the foam with a welcoming slurp. When he looked up he saw that he and the artist were no longer alone, but had been joined by a third party – a man about twenty years older, with about twenty years' more muscle and fat on him as well.

'Poor old Klopsky's been in the wars,' the artist explained to the newcomer, who had drawn up a chair opposite. 'Lungs shot to hell – even the tiniest bit of smoke hurts! Beer's the only thing that will soothe it,' he continued, as if he knew Helmut much better than he did. Where he got the name Klopsky from was a complete mystery.

'Beer's the only thing that will soothe most things!' the stranger chuckled, then clinked the bottom of his glass against Helmut's and bellowed: 'Medicine for what ails you!' and 'Good to know you, friend!' but he did not introduce himself.

The tickle in his throat had died down, but Helmut knew it was still there, lying in wait. It had been there since the summer of 1917. And the stranger was half-right – the medicine was in the drink, though not the beer, rather in the schnapps, which coated his throat warmly. He was not permitted to drink at Mother's, so he always had to leave her house to seek this particular comfort. Still, if things with Sabine went as well as he expected, he would not be there for very much longer anyway.

'Well, then,' the stranger said. 'They got you good, didn't they? Filthy dogs! Sadists! They're screwing us all over, they are, one by one.' He shook his head, but still looked fairly pleased. 'Still, I bet you gave them hell while you were out there, eh?'

And that, thought Helmut, was precisely it. They had given each other hell, all nicely wrapped up, like Christmas, but in shells and canisters.

'Hah,' the fellow went on, 'well, at least you're in one piece. Which is more than you can say for all those other miserable bastards. How old are you, son? Got a wife, kids?'

'He's got a bird, all right,' the artist jumped in. 'On his way to see her right now, as a matter of fact. Least he was till I hauled him in here!'

The older man beamed. 'Well, that's a public service, that is, your good deed of the day!' He lifted his glass to the artist, who then picked up his sketchbook and resumed drawing.

'Good deed?' Helmut echoed.

'By that I meant that you're doing yourself no favours in going to visit a female in your state. Not if you want to impress her, which I'm sure you do. On the other hand, if you were going to give her her marching orders, I'd say you were very well prepared for that indeed – she'll take one look at your mug and happily make her swift exit – by the window if necessary!'

'Here,' said Helmut, 'just what are you saying?' Looking indignantly up at his accuser he saw that there was now a fourth person in their party. This time it was a little girl, twelve years of age or thereabouts, with rosy cheeks and sandy hair cut bluntly across her shoulders. A doll, really.

'Please,' the stranger cried, 'you mustn't misunderstand me! You're obviously a fine fellow, a fine fellow! I only meant that you might not be at your best tonight. Through no fault of your own! But we should all be at our best when we go out into that battleground of the hearts, if we do not want to be defeated. Forgive me, my lad, but you look tired, your skin has a strange hue – sallow is the word for it – plus your eyes are weepy and your cough, well, I'm no doctor, but I wouldn't put money on you. And that's before we even begin to mention the fact that you've been drinking.'

This last point Helmut could not deny. 'I travelled all the way from Hamburg today,' he said meekly in his defence. The appearance of the strange little girl had unnerved him, and the fact that the artist was scrutinising him again did not help matters either.

'Of course, of course. But my point is, should you not wait until you're restored to glory before you approach this maiden? How old did you say you were?'

Crestfallen, Helmut choked back, 'Twenty-six.'

'So young! Yet I'd have guessed *thirty*-six, more like.' He turned to the artist. 'What do you think, Georg? Is this really the best moment for him to be winning hearts?'

The artist, by now deep in concentration, simply shook his head. Helmut noticed that he no longer seemed to be drawing him, but had settled his eye on the little girl instead. She in turn was totally absorbed in skimming the froth off the stranger's beer with her finger.

'Dear boy,' he went on, 'don't despair! It would only be a tragedy if there weren't a simple remedy, but there is. There is much that can be done to improve your health: clean air' – he said without irony – 'and the right medicine.'

'Thank you, but I've probably had enough to drink,' Helmut replied, resolving to leave as soon as he had finished his beer, or until he had spilled this one all over the bench too.

'A small misunderstanding, I don't mean that,' the stranger said. 'You see, war takes all the youth and vigour out of a man. For that you need a stronger medicine than anything they sell here. Something pure and good, and delicate and kind. Something that will make you feel a man again.'

He drew back from the table a few inches, patted his lap, and allowed the little girl to climb up onto it. As if a button had been pressed on her, she broke into a tentative smile. 'Lovely, isn't she! A perfect little snowdrop.'

The artist tsked; she had ruined his composition. 'Ah, well,' he said, 'I was nearly done anyway.'

Helmut felt his whole body tremble and shudder, as if those dreadful butterflies had suddenly awoken. He lurched towards the artist and grabbed the sketchbook from him, and in doing so saw what had been in the young man's mind when he'd spied him across the carriage. The sketch was of a man seated, his two feet planted firmly on the ground and his legs long and thin, while the top half of him was swollen and contorted, a miserable assembly of bulges and shadows – the overall effect of which was rather arachnoid. Yet the body had only been sketched rudimentarily, for what the artist had most focused on was Helmut's face, which came across as a mask on a head that was too big for it, so that the whole thing had an air of horrible caricature. And he'd had to make that face broad, too, because upon it he'd laid every single line, spot and disfiguring mark that Helmut had ever acquired, as well as a few that he had not. The eyes bulged, rheumy and bloodshot, above a sharp nose and thin, weak lips, and these had been accentuated by the use of a heavy lead pencil, while denying Helmut's likeness any shading or nuance. Here he was a mere outline of a man, a canvas for the ravages of the world. How cruel of him! How unjust! Should not an artist represent life? This was not life, but death. And now Helmut saw that he was Death.

Worse still. At the foot of the figure the artist had added another, that of the girl. She was sitting cross-legged, but due to the lack of perspective in the drawing appeared to be just hovering there, as if on an invisible flying carpet. She was gazing up at the viewer wide-eyed, those eyes almost as large as his, but somehow more radiant; her small hands and straw-like hair he had captured perfectly. *Discharged Soldier and Child Prostitute.* The artist had not yet labelled his work, but Helmut knew what it was.

He leapt to his feet, slamming the offending image on the sodden tabletop, and lurched at the artist, who evaded his grasp. Instead he grabbed at the stranger, managing to take hold of his coat collar, and then he pulled him around the bench by it, as a teacher does the ear of a naughty boy. The little girl had tumbled off the man's lap and, having landed like a cat on the filthy floor, crawled under a table to watch.

'Friend, please!' her pimp gasped. Paralysed by surprise at the turn of events, he allowed Helmut to pull him through the door and to throw him into the snow outside. It was still drifting down in gentle whorls as Helmut laid into the man. Pleading no more, he merely groaned and clutched at himself, as if that might be enough to hold his body together. Behind them followed the artist and the child.

'Good God, Klopsky!' the artist cried. 'What's come over you? Have you gone mad?'

The little girl stood a few inches behind him, and it wasn't until Helmut turned from his first victim and began to advance towards the artist that she abandoned her position and, though the snow swallowed up her feet, ran silently into the night. Helmut beat the artist with great concentration, flecking the ground red with him, but he had already expended much of his fury on the older man and was soon tired. He scraped at the dregs of his energy to produce a final crunch to the artist's ribs, paused to orient himself a moment and then made off in the direction of the station.

When the bar was out of sight he slowed his gait and, as his breath slowed with it, the remarkable clarity of the night flooded in. He was on the bridge above the station now, suspended over the tracks, with window-lights everywhere punching neat holes in the darkness. He looked for the girl's footprints in the snow, but none seemed small enough. The air was thin and sharp – glassy, even – and he wondered why he was not feeling it in his lungs. Sweat was pouring off him, so Helmut took off his coat and immediately it stilled, seeming to form a thin layer of ice across his body. By the time the next train arrived he was shivering, but this was better than putting back on the heavy, smoky overcoat. He plonked himself down in the otherwise empty carriage and let the coat slip to the ground beside him. It was late, well past the time Sabine would be having her supper, yet he knew she would still be awake. They had once been engaged – almost – and she would have to receive him whatever the hour.

Helmut leaned his head back a moment, then sat up again. He took out his handkerchief and issued a mighty cough that brought up an impressive gob of sputum. There, that was it. It was done. He patted himself down, tugged at his cuffs and wiped the snow off his trousers. Then he used the clean edge of his handkerchief to polish each shoe before folding it back up and sliding it into his breast pocket again, so that only a tiny white triangle showed. After that he got out his comb and, tilting his head carefully, as if it were a valuable antique, began combing his hair – every single strand back into its proper place. Only when he was sure that everything was in order again did he turn to look at his reflection in the window, and see how cool and glossy and black it was against the brilliant night.

3

August

She had just finished the breakfast washing-up, and was carrying the tub to the door to toss it in the drain outside, being very careful not to slosh the dirty water on the floor or on her feet. She had not even reached the door when the incident occurred. Before it, she had been wearing a light cotton kimono, a small apron around her waist, and a polka-dot scarf on her head to keep the hair out of her face, but she liked the way it looked on her, too. She wore white ankle socks and underpants, and no bra. After the incident, only her socks remained. Everything else had vanished in the light. It had seared through the house, prickling her all over, but her eyes especially. For a moment after opening them she thought she had gone blind; it was weirdly gloomy, even though the ceiling and walls had been ripped away. The darkness was in the sky itself, as if night had lost its way and stumbled into day. Around her were heat and rubble and the splinters of things torn. She gazed down at her body. There was no pain there; she seemed unhurt, and could move with ease. She left the kitchen, passed the remains of the room in which her parents had been sitting, and went out into the street.

He cannot remember what reason she gave for not going into the wreckage to search for them. Did she give a reason? Strange that she should confess to leaving her parents behind without offering an explanation. Of course, even if they had survived the blast, they probably wouldn't have lasted very long. Most of the souls in that neighbourhood had already perished. Still, she should have stopped to check.

Something drifts into his consciousness. A scent. Sesame, burning.

He goes into the kitchen. His wife is frying rice balls made from yesterday's leftovers. They are covered in sesame seeds and crisping in a thin sheet of oil. She presses them with the back of a spoon, as if in gentle admonition, and they sizzle a little more fiercely. She seems to derive some satisfaction from that.

She sees him watching and says, 'They'll cook quicker that way.'

'There's no rush,' he replies.

'You have to get to work, don't you?'

'I'm not running late.'

'Then take your tie off before you eat, you'll splash it. Sit down.'

He sits and begins to undo his tie, as if he has just returned home rather than being about to leave it – a glitch in time. She hands him a bowl of broth, a smaller one of pickled root vegetables and grilled eel. Then she whisks the tie away, hanging it over his briefcase near the door, and returns to the stove to retrieve the rice balls. 'Ah!' she exclaims, folding herself down opposite him, and only rests there for a second before leaning forward to pour his tea. He notices, for the first time, that there is a crease down the middle of her forehead; it is still there now that she has sat upright again.

They married six months after Japan's surrender, and now another six years or so have passed. It is remarkable how little he feels for her, or her for him. They do not ask anything of each other except to be allowed to get on with their lives, and this they do without exchanging a word on the matter. For this he is grateful. The fact that two people can exist in the world like this is barely comprehensible to him. He feels that there is no sense in harmony, that serenity is not theirs to own. But he supposes a lot of people feel like that.

She did not recount what she had seen in the street. There was no need. Rubble, wood, bodies. A lot of ash, or something like ash. Splinters. Fires. Vomit. She vomited too.

'Standing or did you sit down to do it?' the doctor inquired.

'I stopped. I bent over. I was shaking, I got it all over my feet. But in the stream it came off.'

The stream was behind the cluster of houses where she lived. It had been her instinct to jump into it.

'Is that because you felt like you were burning?' asked the doctor.

'Yes, everything was burning,' she replied.

It was a shallow stream, which was just as well, because otherwise she would have drowned. She let the stream carry her along, half-floating, half-sprinting, her feet brushing over the pebbles on its bed. They were cold − even colder than the water − and hard, but touching them did not cause any pain. It felt good to have them there. Above, the air was warm and cloudy and eerily still. The stones seemed a kind of armour for another world secured safely beneath them. She couldn't enter that world, but just knowing that it was there was a comfort.

She did not know how long she was in the water: not long. After a while a pair of strong arms threaded through hers and pulled her out. She lay on the grass, convulsing and gasping like a fish. She vomited again, then passed out.

He straightens his tie and picks at a sesame seed that has become stuck between his teeth. A gust of air seems to blow the train towards him; it slides to a halt at his feet and he steps inside. Doing so he notices how one of his shoes has a scratch across the toe, spoiling the leather, as if he had walked through a thicket. He has no idea how, in the area in which he lives, that could have happened, but it has and there is nothing to be done about it. He takes a seat − one of the good things about living so far from the city is that he always gets a seat − fingers the scratch on his shoe, and settles in for the 52-minute journey.

He had not learnt about the bomb until several hours later. He'd been in his parents' village in the hills, recovering from a bout of typhoid. The illness had interrupted his medical training and he had been sent home to recover. On 6 August he was still weak, and had slept all morning. It was not until noon, when his mother came in to wake him, that he learnt what had happened in the valley below. He asked his parents if they thought he should return to the city to help. His father immediately replied that he should; his mother said only that it was his decision, but he could see that she didn't want him to go. Both of them wept when he left the next day. They hoped to be one of the families in the village that had not lost a son.

She awoke on the floor of a makeshift camp. The men who had rescued her seemed to have disappeared, but she thought they must be soldiers, as there were a lot of soldiers around, trucked in from happier places. Other citizens occupied the mats around her. Some of them couldn't lie down because of their injuries, so they sat hunched over, beetle-like. Some were silent, like her; others wept or called out.

Slowly, her body returned to her, but it did not come gently, for it seemed to carry with it the pain of others. The nausea returned too, but her throat was dry, and nothing came. Her head ached as if the blinding light had been trapped inside it and was now searching for a way out again. She rolled to the side to retch, and in her convulsions her bowels emptied, like the rest of her, to accommodate new pains. The fact that she was not the only one who lost control of herself did not diminish her shame. A soldier came over, cupped her head in his enormous palm and, not speaking to her or even looking her in the eye, dripped water into her mouth until she went limp as if to say, enough, though it was not.

The next day she was transported to a larger aid station, where she received treatment. The journey – all jolts and shudders – was a torment, but as soon as she was deposited on her new mat she felt a sense of calm and wellbeing. 'I'm okay,' she told the doctors, 'I feel fine,' but they would not let her leave. So she lay there picking at her skin and pulling at her hair. It came out easily, but she could not stop.

He is about ten minutes into his journey when a woman sits down next to him, rather than in one of the empty seats opposite; she too would like to face forward. He didn't catch sight of her before she sat down and now it would be improper to try to see her face, so instead he glances at her legs, at the hem of her pink dress and her handbag propped up on her knees. She wears a light fragrance, something floral rather than chemical, and it seems to suit her even though he has nothing to go on but the contours of her presence. At the next stop a man gets on and sits opposite them but, contrary to expectation, doesn't raise his eyes to look at her. The newcomer is in the perfect position for a surreptitious peek and yet does not hazard a try. There is something rather contemptuous, he thinks, rather cowardly, about this refusal to encounter beauty. This thought comes to him undiluted by pity, so it does not linger long.

His first patient in the tents was a middle-aged man, but he had died after only a few minutes. 'Don't take it personally, kid,' the supervising doctor said, putting his hand on his shoulder. 'There are plenty more.'

She was his second. Twenty-nine years old, she said, though she looked older. Married, but alone – her husband had vanished on one of the China campaigns. No children that she would admit to. She told him how the last thing she remembered, as she took the dirty water to the door, was the sound of cicadas, and he lied and told her how he'd heard them that warm morning too, when really he'd slept through the whole thing. She lay serenely as he examined her, first her front and then her back, helping her to roll onto her side. She didn't make a sound then, but when he laid the sheet back over her she winced. You have been quite badly burnt, he said, pointlessly, and immediately regretted it.

The few nurses on duty were all busy, so he dressed her wounds and attended to her himself. He took her temperature – it was high, nearly 41 – and a blood sample. He would have liked to sit by her side, but she was tired, and more patients were arriving by the minute. Soon he was assigned six more.

She lay there waiting, like all the others, for her doctor to visit her again. The time between each of these encounters was dangerous, because it was the space into which death might slip. She knew he could see her from where he was in the far corner of the room. He had other patients to look after. She willed his return, but it was hard, the strength of her gaze too weak, and so she stared at the ceiling instead, the layered canvas of a hastily erected tent. When eventually he came back it was with a senior doctor, so he did not sit by her mat or hold her hand while pretending to take her pulse, as he often did. Now with his superior beside him he stood at the end of her mat, discussing her case. In that moment the pain flared up even more fiercely than before, as if responding to a rollcall. But she did not want to give a performance. She shifted a little, her hand limp beside her, and smiled wanly. She did not look at them and she did not speak.

He is jolted out of his reverie by the flash of the morning sun swinging across his face. Then the train turns again and the light leaves his eyes, allowing him to come back to his recollections. They are fine and beautifully polished, for every morning he turns them over and over again.

A few days later it was Nagasaki. They were not permitted to tell the patients, but word got out anyway. Some of the doctors left to attend to the new site of catastrophe, and it was expected that their experience of this strange kind of burn would help the next round of survivors. As a student from the prefecture, however, he was instructed to stay behind.

He had still not quite recovered from the typhoid. He had a slight fever, it hurt when he coughed, and dragging himself from patient to patient was an effort. It was one of the reasons he had begun sitting down next to them as he did his rounds, and now they expected it. With his superior gone he could spend more time at her side. Her hand burned in his; it was uncomfortable for them both, but they persisted.

She was getting sicker. Her temperature rose as her white blood cell count plummeted. Some of her wounds had begun to ulcerate, she could not keep food down and her hair was rapidly falling out. When he was not there she fingered the prayer beads that had belonged to an old man who had succumbed the day after the blast; when he approached he saw her slip them around her wrist and hold out her palm for his.

He had heard that, in an effort to keep their patients alive, some doctors were attempting blood transfusions. But his camp did not have the facilities or the reserves for that. He had already donated blood, and as far as he knew it had been used despite his illness, because the need was judged greater than the risk.

He did not speak to her very much; she seemed to have trouble concentrating and rarely replied. Much later he realised that this should not have made any difference.

She slumped further into herself, sinking away from him and into a deep sleep. He stood, walked to the storage cupboard and extracted from it a glass syringe. He dropped it into his smock, retired to the water closet, put the needle to the crook of his elbow and drew from it a quotient of blood. Arterial, red, rich. It looked healthy – it did not seem to have come from him at all. He felt it to be something sacred, miraculous.

She was still sleeping when he returned. Pretending to minister to another patient, he waited until one of the nurses had passed and then went to sit beside her. Under the sheet he slipped the needle into her arm and depressed the syringe.

She did not stir, but she did not die either. It was as close to a transfusion as she would get.

He was sure he was doing the right thing.

She recalled the pebbles, picket fences, her father's ashtray, chipping a sake bottle that had been in her family for centuries, and waiting for her husband to return. Now she was waiting again, for her doctor, for anyone. She imagined her husband's disappointment, were he to return and come to her bedside, only to find that she had died, or was about to. In the meantime pain would come in waves, burning and throbbing through her body, exploring her. Her chest was the worst, though; it was the place where the pain had staked itself permanently.

She knew he was trying to make her well again. The first two times he came to inject her she had pretended she was asleep. She had felt the warmth of it, not like any injection she'd had before. The third time she'd opened her eyes, and was astonished to see that it was blood that was going into her. 'It's mine,' he'd said, 'it's good for you.' After that she watched him intently as he injected her, under the covers, out of sight. She knew: he had singled her out for this special treatment, but she did not know why – she was not special, nor very beautiful. Especially not now. It revolted her, the flow of this tepid sap, but she could barely separate this feeling from her general sense of disgust with herself and with the world. He was young and, she suspected, didn't know what he was doing. But she felt an obligation to stay alive, to not squander what he had given her.

He steps off the train. There is a light wind and the sun is still sitting low in the sky. As the train departs in one direction and the passengers in the other, he stands for a moment on the platform, his breath shallow, picks up his briefcase and the memory of her, and leaves the station.

That day was unusual because there had been children at the camp. Not only as patients, but healthy ones, unaffected by the blast. They were from Kobe and had travelled with their mother to find their father, an actor whose troupe had been booked for two performances in Hiroshima. The children were young and tried to clamber over him; their small dog ran through the camp, stopping to sniff at the patients, until the supervisor caught it and tied it up outside. He used the distraction to steal away into the water closet to fill another syringe. When he emerged a minute later, a colleague was standing nearby, apparently waiting for him. She had gone, his colleague said, and for a moment he thought she had only been discharged, and the feeling was one of acute disappointment, even betrayal.

He went over to her mat. Someone had drawn the blanket up to cover her head. He noticed there were white dog hairs on it; she must have been visited by the creature before she passed away. And what he remembers above all is her cupped hand, those white hairs, and the weight of his blood in his pocket. Warm but growing cold, of no use to anyone now.

4

The mouleuse

Balma, France, 1855

Today my wife began work on a new one. An artillery officer, who has been discharged mostly intact. He is uncommonly tall, she says, and when he lies down on the table his feet will hang over the edge, he will be uncomfortable. But then it is not usually a comfortable business. Though she tries to put the patients at ease, she is not always successful. Some of them don't want to be touched or even looked at, and especially not by a woman. But this one, she says, seems to be quite relaxed.

About this new patient there is not yet much more to tell. It was only their first meeting, and the first is just for talking, her task being simply to gain the patient's confidence and to explain the procedure to them. Many of them do not know a thing about *moulage* and have no idea what they will be subjected to. They imagine that if it is in aid of medicine then it will be a medical procedure. They are here on their physician's orders and have little say in the matter. So it is much better for everyone if they trust their *mouleuse* from the very start.

She begins by showing them a complete wax mould. She always uses the same one, a life-sized relief of a baby's face framed in a lacy bonnet. The child is rosy-cheeked and has no apparent afflictions – it is beautiful and serene, and seems entirely healthy. She has chosen the least repulsive and most tender model she has ever made. She does not tell them that it is the death mask of our son, Éric.

'See,' she tells them, 'if a tiny baby can do it, so can you.' The lie hurts only her, I think.

Then she explains to them the process. She warns them that the skin will feel hot under the hardening plaster, that it will tighten. Those who are having their face cast find it the most difficult. They will likely have their eyes and mouth covered, in which case the patient often feels like they are suffocating. It takes a while for the plaster to dry, and in that time they will be inclined to dwell excessively on the misery of their situation, or to panic. Sometimes they weep. Of course, this is a disaster for the moulding process – for the face crumples, and the plaster will not harden properly while fresh tears infuse it; in that case she will have to start all over again. So she does her best to distract them. She will talk to them, read them stories or sing. If their faces are free – that is, if some other part of them is under plaster, or she is only touching up the original mould – she might also show them paintings and picture books, and engage in conversation with them. They may discuss anything they wish, she says. If they want to talk about their affliction, she will indulge them, but most often they do not. Usually they would rather talk about anything but. With their disfigurements covered up and bound by several layers, sealed away from the world and somehow separate from them, they are able to think about other things.

'What's wrong with this one?' I ask.

'Syphilis.'

'What stage?' I have learnt much about such afflictions since my wife became a *mouleuse*.

'Secondary.'

I do not ask what part of the body she is working on. I know she has modelled the external genitalia of women before, but I do not imagine her employer, Dr Nadeau, would have her do so on a man.

'How does he look?' I inquire.

'He would be handsome,' my wife replies, 'were it not for the chancre consuming his nose and lip.'

She is doing his face then, thank God.

I am a sculptor, of middling success. And it was I who, long before Léontine became my wife, taught her the moulding technique. My assistant had died, and I needed a replacement who had a knowledge of anatomy and a facility for touch. I found her at the Académie. It was 1850, a year before we were to wed, and the war in the Crimea had not yet begun. If I had known there would be war, and that people would stop commissioning sculptures, preferring to invest their money in arms or squirrel it away instead, I would never have hired a new assistant. But I do not regret my lack of foresight, since with it I would not have met my wife. And because now it is she who puts food on our table.

For just as the war took my livelihood from me, so did it furnish her with a new one. France had not long joined the battlefield when there began a steady stream of soldiers returning disfigured and diseased. Only the physicians could find joy in this, with the opportunities it provided to study and document the ravages of war. But they needed artists capable both of drawing the patients and creating lifelike models of their afflictions. Indeed, I put myself forward, but they only wanted women. A male artist, with brutish, heavy, hairy hands, would resemble too closely the physician himself. Also men were the machinery of war, and these soldiers had had enough of that. A female artist, however, might instead have the qualities of a nurse – compassionate, sensitive, gently bandaging, uttering soothing words and, if young enough, a balm for the eyes as well.

My wife met with the physicians, who examined her folio and made notes on her countenance and voice. 'Melodious,' they noted approvingly, and tested her out on a patient, a young man who'd had half of him blown away – his right leg missing to above the knee and his right arm below the shoulder. His face was as pocked as the moon, by shrapnel and acne both. He had a shattered eardrum, so she'd had to lean in to his left side to communicate with him. He'd spoken very, very softly, almost in a whisper, as if even the sound of his own voice was painful to him, like the pressing on a bruise. I never learnt his name, but if you were to ask my wife I am sure she would recall it. The meeting moved her very deeply. I remember that after she returned home, despite having been chosen for *mouleuse*, she lay sobbing in bed all night.

The next morning her eyelids were a swollen, translucent pink, like something newborn. A woman has qualities of sensitivity and strength, but these are not always held in balance.

Éric died a few weeks later. It was not a great surprise; he had been sickly since the beginning. My wife had produced sketches of him from his birth – three hundred and twenty-one, one for every day of his short life. It was I who suggested, after he joined the angels, that she make a cast of his face. She was resistant at first – I think she did not want to sully the purity of him, to cover him before his time. But after only a day, when all traces of life's essence had finally left him, and his face had perceptibly changed, she understood that she must do it, and quickly too, if she were to capture as much as was dear to her. And with the hope that what she could not capture in the mould she could restore when she manipulated and painted the wax. She took a pair of scissors and, kneeling at the crib, ran her fingers through his spun-gold hair, before carefully snipping from it a precious lock.

At the time I was working on a modest memorial for a town some ten miles away, and from which many young men had left for the war. Three had already perished; one had been sent home. As it was expected there would be more casualties, the mayor asked if I would be able to have a statue ready by the end of the conflict, to honour their fallen sons. Since none of us knew when the end would be, I readily agreed, and set to work immediately. I had a local boy pose for my soldier, and worked upon it in the studio, once a stable, that constitutes nearly half of our home. My statue seemed altogether obscene when set in the same space as the wax face of our boy, which my beloved daubed upon in the corner, trying to colour.

'I can't do it,' she said as I approached. 'I cannot get the hue of his nose. I don't know if I remember it right.' She was mixing the tincture and applying it to a pellet of wax. I bent over her and took her paintbrush, washed it clean and mixed the colour anew, then guided her hand back to the test piece. 'Ah. It's perfect,' she said forlornly. 'I think you remember him better than I do.'

Anton is the artillery officer's name. They have had their second meeting now, in which Léontine was to apply the plaster to his ruined face and so be able to begin the mould. Yet the man was resistant, she told me. Although on their first meeting he had seemed accepting of the process, this time he was decidedly more agitated, and became distressed when she laid out the materials. He complained that his sores felt tender, and was fearful that they would not withstand the heat – that they would blister and suppurate beneath the mould. She suggested placing some protective padding between the lesions and the plaster, but this still worried him, so she proposed working around the sores instead, leaving them exposed to the air, and to mould them later by hand and sight. Yet this would draw out the process by one more session. Would he consent to that? He would, but by the time they reached agreement it was too late to start work for the day. So, she tells me, she will have to go back tomorrow morning.

All this does not seem to bother her. She returns home the next afternoon, seeking me out in our studio. I have just been in the garden to take some fresh air and feel the sun on my face. I have no commissions at the moment, and so spend my time seeking them, or sketching idly. Without a project I cannot settle to anything. If things go on like this I will have to find another vocation. My soldier – for the memorial – stands in the corner of the studio, facing the window as if staring dreamily out of it. The town ten miles away does not want him yet. They are waiting to see how many of their sons fall first.

When Léontine comes in I have returned to the stool at my workbench, and look as if I had been toiling there all day. She comes up behind me and garlands her arms around my neck, her hands meeting over my heart and holding me as if she were my harness, which of course she is. Her cheek presses to mine, and I can feel her drawing breath, drawing in the smell of me. I am smiling, and she knows it. I turn to stand and kiss her, and afterwards she looks at me with warmth and barely concealed pity. Then she undoes herself from me to go and prepare our meal.

I have been feeling tired these days. It makes no sense, since I am barely working. Sometimes I look over the accounts, just to remind myself that we are surviving, that we are in balance. I will not receive the rest of the payment for my soldier until the war ends; sometimes it crosses my mind that they might decide they don't want him after all, and I will be stuck with him. In any case, I must seek out new clients. I must travel from village to town to city to secure new commissions. Though I would rather not have to leave her behind, it could bring us profit. I could make death my business, just as my wife has made disease and deformity hers. It is strange, what artists become in the world.

Now the third meeting is over, and I compel myself to ask her how it went. Since she has been away for most of the day, I imagine her soldier has been uncooperative again, but instead she reports that the meeting went very well. She was able to make a full cast of his face, working around the lesions as planned, and so there are holes in it. But she's pleased with her work, she says; it is a good mould. She has sketched the disfigurement to familiarise herself with its structure, then will reconstruct it with the patient before her. He will see just how she works the wax: how she adds beads to it and moulds them, giving them texture; how she stops them from cracking as they dry. And when the shape is right she will bring her paints and give the whole thing colour and life. She will have to lean in very close to his skin, using her magnifying glass to perceive every detail, and in turn the patient will be able to smell the cooling wax, the lead of the paints.

She'll have to work quickly, too. The physician has just told her that the officer will not receive treatment until the wax model is ready and he has a record of the affliction – until then he does not want the skin clearing up and destroying his sample.

'But that is barbaric,' I say. 'He must be treated immediately!'

'Of course he must. But Dr Nadeau says that in the interests of science —'

'And what does your soldier say about it?' I interrupt.

'He is resigned to his fate. We discussed it today. He takes the view that this is an extension of his duty.'

'The poor fool,' I mutter. Then I ask, although I am not sure why, 'Did you discuss it before or after you applied the plaster?'

'Before,' she replies. 'He wanted to talk while he was still able. I indulged him.'

'Hmm.'

'He is an interesting man. He does not have the character of a soldier, at least not as you would expect it.'

'I would expect a bloodthirsty creature with little compunction about the taking of a human life,' I say.

'I know you would. Which is why I am telling you that he is not like that at all. He has honour in him.'

I look at her in disbelief. Surely she has not forgotten her principles. Surely she has not been completely blinded to the fact that this pitiful creature was still a willing agent of imperialist whims. She does not see this look, as she has turned away to rummage through her food basket. A thick, dusty silence hangs in the air between us.

She asks if I am hungry, if I have eaten today.

I have not. The air seems to have clumped in my throat. 'I was waiting for you,' I reply.

She turns back to me. 'Silly.' She smiles, and kisses my forehead gently, as if I am a child. I soften beneath her touch. Then she says, 'I left you food, and you didn't touch it. You mustn't wait for me next time.'

So, she knew she would be with him all day, and she expects tomorrow will be the same.

'I won't wait,' I agree, drawing away. My mind spins into an imagined future, in which I am eating alone in our dark, cool kitchen, while my wife shares a meal with her soldier. I see him propped up in bed, her by his side. On the bedclothes the books she was using to entertain him. A bandage around his head and an officer's cap perched on top of it.

Of course not. Why would he be in bed? There is nothing wrong with him, save for his disease.

And so the picture scrambles. Now he is sitting at a table, and she is opposite. A small selection of dishes lies between them. He sits up quite naturally, if a little too stiffly — he is a soldier and an aristocrat, after all. Still, I cannot imagine his face, so I put his head in a plaster hood that covers everything, including his eyes, ears and nostrils, but leaves the mouth free. A dark hole into which he carefully inserts his food. Or she inserts it. Leaning forward, to assist.

It is not a likely scenario, I suppose. Truly, I cannot imagine their meetings. She tells me about them but truly, I cannot imagine them.

All the great failures of men stem from a failure of the imagination.

She can see that I am vexed, that I am not present with her in the moment, but lingering in others.

'I'm telling you, he is not as you would expect.'

'Then explain to me,' I say, 'how a man who rushes off to murder his fellow men, and who finds his relief between the legs of a desperate whore, is not as I would expect.'

She's alarmed. I know that my voice is raised, and it has destroyed the sanctity of our home, but I do not care enough. *Good*, I think, *let her look at the truth, and let it burn a little.*

'He is uniquely sensitive,' she says. 'He laments the carnage; he abhors war.'

'All soldiers love war, up until the point that it destroys them. It is only because his destruction is dishonourable that he loathes it now.'

'No, he told me he formed his opinions much earlier than that.'

'But still he rushed off to the orgy.'

'He did not have a choice. His family forced it upon him.'

I lower my voice, finally finding clarity in the truth of my argument. It is a sonorous bell that cleaves the air between us. 'Every man has a choice,' I say.

Yet she will not yield. 'Not every man. Did you have a choice when you made your soldier that would celebrate the slaughter?'

I protest that it is not the same. That I have – that I still have – a family to support. That I have not killed anyone.

'He has not killed anyone, either.'

'Ah, that is what he told you?'

Her eyes fill with tears, and I know that if she begins to cry I will not be able to bear it. 'I am not attacking you, my love.'

'But you are attacking,' she says, and this I cannot deny. I feel a rage inside me, against death, against the Emperor, against the manipulations of men. Against those who kill in the name of glory, and who all the while cannot see that life itself is the ultimate glory. I long for absolute purity, and love, and she is my only source of it. I would like to hold her but she has turned away from me.

I go outside. The sun covers me but offers no comfort.

The town ten miles away, I am told, has lost two more men. They were in the same regiment, stationed at the Sea of Azov. A bomb exploded nearby; one was killed instantly and the other lingered in agony for several hours before succumbing to his injuries. In our town, one of the veterans has already returned – Michel, the son of the cobbler Frédéric. I saw him in the street. He limped past me, avoiding my eye. He knows my position, just as I know his. And then – God help me – I understood that in his suffering is my vindication.

We must make a new Éric. The world must be populated anew, with people who have no hate in their hearts.

I have a little, but it is the right kind, and it will pass.

I can see, when she returns the next day, that she is tired. Though all is forgiven, she does not approach me, instead waits for me to come to her.

I am coming to her. I am falling at her feet and kissing her hands. Her hands smell of wax, and they feel like wax, too – warm and clammy, like wax that is half-set, and may still be prodded and moulded. I let them go again.

'Just a moment, my love,' I mumble, before my legs have carried me outside, to the pond down near the big oak, and I have plunged my hands into the cool water.

The ducks scatter in alarm, all feathers and feet.

At once I feel better. She's watching me from the doorway, and I beckon her over. 'Here,' I say, taking her hands and guiding them beneath the surface, 'isn't it nice?'

She laughs. 'What an eccentric I have married!' And the spectres of exhaustion and disease lift from her. The ducks sit at the opposite edge of the pond, not quite ready to get back in, for they have not yet judged me so harmless.

I lie down on my back, one arm stretched out, and she accepts the invitation and nestles herself in it. I feel as though I have recaptured her heart, and that we are starting anew. With my other hand I move to caress her belly, but as it moves towards her sex, there her hands stop mine, and now there is a resistance in her. She does not fit with me any more, she will not be persuaded.

'Not now, not here. I'm so very tired,' she says, lifting herself out and away from me and straightening her smock. So, we are both tired. Yet we cannot find a way to create a new vitality between us. I follow her to the house at a distance, then also at a distance sit and watch her prepare our supper. As I watch her hands touch the meat, I wonder if I will be able to eat it.

The next evening I ask her if the work is finished and she says it is, almost. Tomorrow will be the last session with the officer. She has only to put the finishing touches on the mould and then she will present it to the physician, who will examine it beside the patient. It must be perfect; there must not be a perceptible difference between the two. If the physician is not happy with her work then she will have to continue until she gets it right.

'But you are happy with it, aren't you?' I say. 'You believe it will be finished?'

She is certain, yes. She is proud of this one.

'And then he will receive treatment?'

He will.

'What will the treatment be? How will they cure him?'

It is better, she assures me, if I do not know the details.

But I doubt it can be much worse than what I am thinking now. We are in bed and she is lying on her stomach, her head turned to face me. I will her to open her eyes and look at me, but she does not, even though she is not yet asleep. The effort of a few tiny muscles could save us, but she has concentrated her gaze so much on this man that she has nothing left for me. What does she see, I wonder, in her mind's eye? The sores on him, or the texture of the surrounding skin that betrays his once-good looks? His eyes twitching beneath her as she smooths the wet plaster over him? She has been asked by some patients to conceal their identities – that when she models their face she should make slight changes to certain features, so that they would not be recognisable. The curve of a nose or brow, the fullness of the lips or the colour of the eyes. For most, it is the only image of them that will endure into the future – usually, they are simple folk who will never be photographed or painted. They know that the bodily humiliation they suffer will be eternal, unless they can separate themselves from it now. And then there are those who allow her to depict them as they are, for they believe that if she alters one tiny thing about them, then their illness will, in its posterity, be the sole enduring feature of their unhappy lives.

It is ugly, this world. She is immersed in it more deeply than I, yet it contaminates us both. If only she would open her eyes. *Oh, God, I do not want to be in it alone.*

My hand slips under her nightdress, too swiftly this time for her to stop it. It is already on her pudenda. She squirms away, suddenly wide awake, but it is too late.

I have perceived something strange about her sex, which is coarse and bristled under my touch. We pull away from each other, like Adam and Eve shamed.

I ask her what she has done.

'Nothing,' she says, 'please, it's nothing.'

I am thinking, *She is diseased* – and then I realise that it is not a new thought after all.

'Show me what is wrong with you.' My voice quivers deeply. I fear I am about to vomit. But it does not stop me from grabbing at her and tearing at her nightdress. She tries to fall off the bed, her weight propelling her away from me, but I am holding on tight and now she is half-suspended, hanging over the edge, and as she endlessly tumbles I catch a glimpse of her sex, and I can see what she has done.

'You have shaven yourself!'

And with that I release her and she drops to the floor, and I follow, straddling her, and I lift up her nightdress to examine her properly. She has removed all the hair from her pubis, as close to the skin as possible. I prise open her legs – she is entirely passive now – and inspect her. Apart from the shaving, her sex is as it should be. I stand up – I have been sitting on her legs quite heavily – and beg her to tell me why she has done this, and to be quick about it, before I lose my mind.

Léontine is suddenly calm. She needed the hair for her model, she says. 'I could not ask you, of course. I could not ask anyone.' I do not reply. She goes on. 'It is not the same, hair from other parts of the body. Even from the armpit, the quality and texture is quite different. You know that. One can see it immediately.'

So, she has modelled his cock also. She has added to the figure these bits of herself, pressed them into the wax, one by one, all around the model of the diseased organ, all in the name of verisimilitude. And that bastard physician, knowing that she was a married woman, allowed it.

'You must not think that I touched it,' she continues. 'I swear to you I did not, I would not.' She gets up, brushes the tears on her face, glistening.

'But you are happy with your work,' I declare bitterly. 'That is what you said.' I regret treating her as I did, and as I am. It must stop. I forbid her to return.

But she shakes her head, resolved. 'I have to. He will not be treated until I finish the *moulage.*'

'You are not going back.'

'My love, it is just one more day.'

'I forbid it, I forbid it!' I cry.

But she is too clever for me. 'If I do not go, I will not be paid.'

'Then go,' I mutter, although we both know that her logic is stronger, and my resolve more fragile. To stop me, to prevent me from plunging off an abyss of my own making, she retreats from the scene. She knows that I can only destroy myself in her presence. She has gone into the studio, and closed the door behind her.

My guilt prevents me from following her, but I cannot stay in the bedroom, in its accusing disarray. So I venture into the night, and begin walking. The sky is a dark, luminescent blue, like the surface of a lake, rippled only by the sound of crickets in the brush. Soon I have left the township, the last of the lights, the soft braying of horses, the cobbled path. I am alert to everything – the whole world seems to twitch with life – except my own body, which is only the instrument through which everything else is measured. I walk as if in a trance, paying no heed to the route I am taking, yet miraculously I do not lose my way; at dawn I realise I have not wandered very far, only circumnavigated the town, and I am now approaching the point of my departure.

The following month I see a strange thing. I am in the eleventh town on my route, and several miles from home – the furthest I will go before I turn around and make my way back again. It has been a moderately successful excursion. Five of the communes I visited have expressed interest in my memorials, and two have definitively commissioned one. One mayor asked me to return when they have done the final tally of their losses. It was a risky enterprise, hiring a cart and driver to take me around, but it has already paid off. The cart carries my soldier, an example of my fine craftsmanship. I arrive in a new place and, with the help of the driver, prop it up on the ground for all to see. Then, once word has spread, I take him to the local authorities, to canvas support for a commission. Most communes do not have any kind of statue in them, yet all of them have at least one woman who gazes at my soldier and sees her fallen son. In the smaller villages, I offer them a more modest memorial – a bronze plaque or a cross.

This town, however, is quite large, and I have high hopes. I would like to return to my wife and be able to tell her that my long absence has been justified by no less than three commissions. Her work for the hospital continues, but is less frequent now that they have accumulated a fine gallery of afflictions.

Here, though, there is competition for our attention. An exhibition organised by a local doctor has opened in a private building off the main street, preceded by the tantalising warning that it is not suitable for women or children. There are nevertheless a good number of women and children in the queue. I join it − normally there is nothing at all going on in such towns − although I know what to expect. The exhibition is of medical curiosities, and is at first sight rather dull. Apart from the skeleton of a two-headed piglet, and a series of wax reliefs showing the development of a chick inside an egg (this I have never seen before), it is mostly unidentifiable body matter in jars and sketches of the deformed. There are just two daguerreotypes, one of which is of a veiled woman whose only exposed feature is a bloated foot. The other is of a seated soldier with a missing leg. It is nothing remarkable; in a large town such as this there will likely be one or two of them limping around, anyway.

The strange thing, though, is not here but further along, in an antechamber behind a velvet curtain. A man at the door is turning away the women and children. With the men present he directs their attention to a small sign: 'Due to the artistic worth of this exhibition and its value for medical advancement, we politely request for entrance to this section a small but fair donation.' I suspect I know what I am going to see. Nevertheless, I drop a coin into the hand of the doorman, and he lifts the curtain to let me through.

Sure enough, it is a room of wax studies, as well as several lewd lithographs of dubious scientific value. Inside the room with me is a cohort of well-dressed gentlemen, each of them lingering thoughtfully over the displays. There are many *moulages*, perhaps forty – an impressive collection in any case. I walk down a row of pustulous and disintegrating faces, stopping at a wax hand that, not very well preserved, is webbed in fine cracks, like a Japanese ceramic. Some of the *moulages* are cold and blank, clearly modelled off cadavers; others are so lifelike as to be terrifying. One in particular catches my eye – the face of a man with sores across his nose and mouth. The note says simply 'syphilis', with a number beside it that is meaningless to me. The man's eyes are closed, unlike some of the models here, which have glass eyes that reflect, to a remarkable extent, glimmers of hope and anguish. He seems to be calm and sentient. Not sleeping, but rather deep in restful thought.

Of course, I do not know for sure that it is her officer. It is only that I feel it must be. I peer more closely at the wax; it is a recent model of exceptional quality, the colouring beautifully done, with the clippings of fine hair from a young child's head inserted for the eyelashes. This is my wife's technique, and though it is not uniquely hers, I feel certain that it is her work I am looking at now.

As I examine it, other men pass behind me, looking over my shoulder and, not perceiving anything of especial interest, move on again.

It is a pity, for it is a very fine piece of work.

Of course, I have not forgotten that another piece of him was also moulded. And that it too might be in this room.

I take one last look at the man. It is impossible not to feel mercy and pity for him. I wonder if she has captured the essence of him, or if she has disguised it a little.

Across the room, where the gentlemen are gathered, I can see there are three phalluses. I go over, take a glance, narrow it down to a possible two, and move on quickly, for propriety's sake.

I will never tell her I was here.

5

Moon tide

Near Faizabad, Afghanistan, 1986

In two hours the moon would rise, chalked over the contours of the valley. Now it was crouched low behind a series of jagged rocks, waiting for the last glimmer of heat and light to recede.

'It's made of ice,' Vitya once told him. 'All ice. That's why it's waiting. If it comes out before the sun has gone it'll melt.'

That was a long time ago, when they were boys. After that Pyotr started paying attention to the moon, imagining it fearful as it hid from the bullying sun. On cloudy days he thought about how hard it must be for the moon to determine where the sun was hiding, and when it would be safe to come out. Perhaps the moon could sense the sun's heat, could feel its surface begin to slip and slide and melt, and know when to withdraw. And then one day Pyotr saw the moon in broad daylight, a white fingerprint on the blue, a mark of complete defiance. He had run to Vitya's, dragged him out of his home and into the street and shown him, 'Look!' And Vitya had said: 'Ach, that's not the moon. That's just its decoy. To confuse the sun. The real moon is hiding, probably.'

That was when Pyotr realised his best friend was full of shit.

In the twilight he walked over to the camp and caught sight of Vitya squatting on the ground. As he came closer he saw that he was busy sloshing water from the canteen into the tin cans from which they'd all just been eating.

Oh God, look at him, he can't be left alone for a second. He's wasting water. We'll all die out here, die of fucking thirst...

'Vitya!' he hissed. 'Viktor Alexievich! What the fuck do you think you're doing?'

'Just washing,' Vitya replied, and Pyotr saw then that he was using his fingernails to scrape clean the insides of the cans.

'Oh Lord, Vitya...you fucking idiot, the whole point of the cans is that you throw them away afterwards. Fucking hell, what is wrong with you, man...'

He took the can off him and placed it with the others, stacked clean in the fading light.

Vitya looked up slowly, and the line of his mouth curved a little, almost into a smile but not quite. He nodded as if he understood. Then he picked up another dirty can, spat into it and began to wipe the inside with his shirt-tail instead.

Pyotr stared at him, yanked the can away and after a moment's reflection decided not to give him a slap. *He's getting stupider by the day. God preserve us, if this goes on, that's it, I'm not fucking kidding, that's it.*

They had been at their post for almost a fortnight. In the hills below the mujahedin went about their business; there had only once been an exchange of fire. The silence of night in the mountains was different from the silence of day, which was filled with static. Or perhaps not static, but the hum of the wings of the millions of flies that formed reckless spirals around the soldiers, and everything else that stank, too. Once a week a chopper would bring supplies and take away the sick and the dead — five hundred cans of cabbage soup for one body. In the minutes before he fell asleep, after the sleepy chatter of his comrades had died down, Pyotr wondered whether he would ever make it onto that chopper. He vaguely hoped for a fever, or a mild bout of dysentery — nothing serious, just enough to earn him a week's rest in Kabul, a week's rest from Vitya.

But he couldn't leave his friend, so that pleasant little fantasy had to shift to accommodate him — Vitya would have to be infected too, and they'd be whisked off into the air together, but then with Vitya along for the ride the fantasy wasn't really so satisfying any more. Pyotr couldn't get sick; he couldn't go off on his own. Without him keeping an eye on things Vitya wouldn't last ten minutes. He didn't have his wits about him, hadn't from the very start, and especially not since being whacked around at training. He'd taken a blow to the head that had sent him straight to the floor, face first, and at least two more kicks had connected with his head after that. Of course, Vitya hadn't done himself any favours trying to avoid conscription in the first place by pretending to be a poof. He'd nearly killed himself trying to prove it — pushed a sock full of dried beans up his arse and after it had expanded yanked it out – he was shitting blood for weeks. It didn't help him any. The recruiters pushed him straight through, but the label stuck. So Pyotr had to keep his distance for the whole of their training – they'd gone in together, but he couldn't be associated with the little fag, and he'd had to leave Vitya to his own devices. Yet Pyotr knew that Vitya understood, that this was just how it was, and so he'd remained apart, collecting his bruises alone, figuring out his own way to lie low. There was no use both of them suffering.

It could have been worse. One guy they knew lopped off his thumb to avoid the draft. That was supposed to exempt you, but he didn't have the 2,000 roubles that would have sweetened the deal and was conscripted anyway. Then the wound became infected and he died before they'd even reached Afghanistan.

Better to do as I did, Pyotr often thought, *and just go with it*. He'd not done too badly. He hadn't been injured and he hadn't fallen into the hands of the enemy, which was far worse. Natalia was still waiting for him, as far as he knew. His parents were proud of him. The troops had just enough food to go round; cannabis, too. The only problem, really, was Viktor. 'Look after my Vityok,' his mother had said to him before they left, out of the earshot of Vitya and his father, while she held Pyotr tight and pressed her wet cheeks against his, confirming the transfusion of responsibility to him.

Some young soldiers were under the impression that the army was the time they could break free from family ties and begin a new life on their own terms, but Pyotr knew better. He understood that it was just an extension of his duty, the duty he was saddled with at birth. It couldn't be otherwise. Still, he dreamt of being stationed somewhere more exciting, where there was some real action and not just endless card-playing and press-ups and short, nervous patrols around the perimeter of the camp, the terrifying and yet boring threat of capture, waiting for the punching bag to free up, its stuffing bulging like a black eye, and hitting it more out of frustration than for exercise, until you were dripping with sweat again. And then the flies.

They took turns to patrol the area. One of the patrols had once been shot at: a shattered collarbone for Danila, but overall a good thing – it broke up the tedium, stopped the boys becoming complacent. Pyotr wondered, if he were about to be captured, whether he would have the guts to top himself before the enemy started work on him. The number of times they'd played at cocking a barrel to their own heads, and still he wasn't sure of the best way to do it. He had to sort it out; he could not be this uncertain. If they came, he wouldn't have long to decide.

Vitya slept on the mat beside him. He was always the first to fall asleep; you could hear it by the whistling through his nose. He would even drop off when you were talking to him, or he to you, at some mysterious, seemingly pre-appointed time. Pyotr marvelled at this, and often wondered, were he to be captured, if Vitya would escape his tormenters by simply fainting away into that deep, intractable sleep. Pyotr looked at the profile of his friend, fuzzy in the blue night, with his childish, clumpy nose and weak chin, and sometimes a fragile pity would rise in him that would show itself at no other point in the day.

With springtime came the bloom of poppies across the valley, and the vanishing of one of their patrols. Three bodies were found three days later. Two were missing hands or feet, the stumps bound in bloody rags; all had been tortured. Well, that was the end of that. They were ordered to abandon camp, and within the week Pyotr and Vitya and the remaining unit were transported back to base.

Pyotr saw the sheer joy on Vitya's face when they learnt they were leaving. Any horror generated by their comrades' fates seemed to have vanished entirely. If Vitya felt any desire for revenge, it didn't show.

'We're not going home, you know,' Pyotr said. 'Just back to base.'

'I know,' Vitya said.

'Then what are you looking so fucking happy for?'

But in his heart he felt it too — a sweet, grateful hope that took the edge off his need for vengeance, and that said to him, Eh. Some you win, some you lose.

And so when a few weeks later a bomb tore off his left leg, he was not very surprised. Some you lose. It was always going to be. That leg that had run and played with him all his life, that had kicked balls and carried him across roads and fields, and that been savaged one summer by Siberian gnats, was never meant to be forever. It had simply been a sham, a dirty trick played on him for so long, only by whom he didn't know.

Vitya had copped it too, although for him it was really just another bump on the head that didn't seem to make much difference. The impact had put him in a coma for a week, and when he came out he was a bit slower, a bit stupider, but then he'd also been recovering from a bout of malaria that had flared up while he was unconscious, and which his body had obviously decided it couldn't be bothered doing anything about. So poor Vitya had emerged weak and dazed, scatty and dumb — and since the doctors hadn't known him beforehand, they assumed this was a dramatic decline. But there wasn't much anyone could do, so they put him down to be discharged alongside Pyotr. No complications.

So, that's all it takes, is it? Pyotr thought. *One boom and they send you home.* Though his leg throbbed terribly, as if it was trying to push blood through an opening that did not exist, and the echo of the throb pounded in his temples, he had the impression that he could still go into combat if need be. They could plonk him down behind some rocks with a Kalash, and he would do his best. Only a fraction of him was missing; the rest still worked perfectly well. You don't get rid of a car just because one of the wheels has fallen off, do you?

Pyotr sat in bed with a notebook propped up against his good leg and began to write. *Mama, we're coming home! Tell Vitushka's family too. We've finished our service, they're letting us go.*

He stopped and stared ahead, his mind suddenly, serenely vacant. A helicopter passed overhead, so loud that it seemed it was about to crash into the roof, but then beat away again. There was a low moan in the ward, a chattering, the rise and fall of footsteps. And then, as if it could not resist joining in, his stump began to throb again. This time, however, it beat not in his head but travelled the length of where his leg had been and then settled, a thick clot of pain, in his absent foot.

Thoughts filtered back in. *There's still a chance, I guess, that we might not make it back. Better not get their hopes up. Wonder if Natalia will cope. Damn. Should've married her...I'll do it when I get back, sort everything out then.*

As soon as Pyotr had been fitted with his new leg they were free to go. The prosthesis was a flimsy thing, but the upgrade would surely be better. At Tashkent airport they waited for the next flight to Kazan. Back across the border it had been the Afghanis all on crutches, and here it was their own. Hundreds of young guys, injured badly enough to be discharged, but not in a way to earn that coveted spell of rehab on the Black Sea. Some had proper prostheses; others did not, and just dragged their injured limbs around with them. 'Wow,' Vitya muttered, 'it's a real epidemic.'

What a fuckwit, Pyotr thought, but he had no strength to reply. His leg, or what was left of it, had consumed all his energy, and what was more, some kind of insect had got into his trouser leg and was biting its way up his thigh. The air was hot and stagnant, filled with the smell of the sweat, disinfectant and DDT that soaked their uniforms, but outside it was much worse – a parody of an oasis, with the haze of heat shifting the sky but promising nothing. Funny how the eighteen snowy winters through which he had lived, which had all seemed so endless then, were now less than a memory. Clammy with blood and perspiration, as if he was composed of nothing else, Pyotr could not even recall how snow crunched underfoot, or how it got into you in the first place. His life had been a silly fairytale, and the mountains, knowing this, obliterated it all.

'Hey, what are you thinking about?' It was Vitya, his voice distant and hollow.

'Same thing as you, probably,' Pyotr replied.

'I'm thinking about the lake. Wondering if my fishing rod is still at home. If we'll go fishing when we get back.'

The lake. Dark as a hole and its depth unknown – Pyotr had always swum in it in mild terror. But he had swum nonetheless, traversing its narrower width, his body warming up quickly with the effort and adrenaline. And the exhaustion and relief, when he finally flopped on the bank, of having survived. He would still be able to make that length, probably – his arms at least were stronger now. But this heaviness in him! Was it only the heat? He knew that if he failed to summon up the strength in his arms then he would sink to the black bottom.

On the ground were their bags, packed full of the booty they'd stolen and bartered for. It weighed a ton, and Pyotr, still unsteady, had to get Vitya to carry the bulk of it. When they finally got the call to board, Vitya hurled the bag over his big stupid shoulders and followed Pyotr onto the plane.

At Kazan the boys spilled wearily out. Many of them kissed the ground of the motherland, despite the difficulty of doing so – they had to lay their crutches aside and descend awkwardly, as if they had no intention of getting up again. Vitya joined them. Pyotr hesitated a moment, wobbled a bit, then simply crossed himself. Just a small cross, and perhaps not done quite right, but it felt good. It was a time to stand tall; he did not want to bow down again.

The cold tingled through him, a distant bell heralding a bodily memory. He relished the feeling for half a minute or so before it began to shiver and irritate him. The sky was slate grey, like a tombstone. He was beginning to wonder if there was any comfort left for him in the world.

The *marshrutka* deposited them five kilometres from their village, at the turn-off from the main road, then drove off into the mist, the sound of its engine remaining far longer than the sight of it. By the side of the road, Vitya picked up the heavier bag, but, seeing that Pyotr had slumped to the ground, put it back down again. 'We gonna wait?' he said.

Pyotr sighed. 'No.' The chances of any cars coming along were slim, but the chances were there, and he didn't want a ride with anyone who was driving into the village. It was bound to be someone they knew, and he needed time to prepare himself for that. He had to prepare Vitya, too. So they would go on foot, making sure not to look weary or pathetic when they approached. Of course, Vitya looked pathetic most of the time – there wasn't much that could be done about that. The main thing was to give the impression that everything was okay.

Pyotr hauled himself up. 'Come on, Vitya, let's walk on the grass...How long has it been since we saw grass?' and led him down into the lush valley at the side of the road, where the mist and dew settled. A little further now and they would not be able to be seen from the road at all. Vitya did not complain. He followed his friend down, like an old packhorse. Hard to believe they were both still young!

After about fifteen minutes Pyotr heard the sound of a vehicle approaching, and stopped still. 'Shh! Wait! Shh!' He could not tell which direction it was going in, but it did not matter. 'Duck! Duck!' He pulled Vitya down onto the moist ground with him and they waited, the damp soaking into them while their heavy breath seeped out. The car passed – it had been leaving the village, after all. A thought entered Pyotr's mind: *I hope that was Papa.*

The next one was not so much a thought as a swell of despair. He was sitting on the wet grass, his leg and his back aching, and everything else consumed by exhaustion. Vitya crouched silently by, awaiting orders.

'Give me the bags,' Pyotr said finally, and Vitya planted them down beside him. Pyotr began rummaging around, not really sure what he was looking for. Vitya didn't ask. Instead he stood up, announced he was going to take a piss, and walked several metres away, so that the silhouette of his body was only barely visible through the gauze of mist. Pyotr's hands stopped still. They had clasped around a pistol. Was it loaded? He couldn't remember. He lifted it out of the bag a little, just enough to be able to check. Four rounds were left. It occurred to him it would be easy to put a bullet in the back of Vitya's head from here. A wholly new idea, which he was surprised he hadn't had before. Put him out of his misery, save his mother the pain of seeing her son like this. Tell everyone he died back there, a hero. There might be something rather grand about that.

But then who would believe it? Our Vitya, a hero? Don't make me laugh! Not even his daft old mama would buy that. She would ask for the body, she would make a fuss. She would plead with Pyotr for help, then plague him for the rest of his life.

Dammit, what's taking him so long? He's standing there like a dummy, almost like he wants me to shoot him.

Ach, it was a stupid thought anyway. Without Vitya, who would carry the bags? Pyotr held the pistol a little longer, then pushed it back down to the bottom of the rucksack. He leaned back on his palms, pressing his fingers through the green and into the soft earth, the dirt crawling up beneath his fingernails. Vitya was still standing in the same spot, his back to him. He seemed to be gazing into the mist. There was a tranquillity about him that made Pyotr nervous, as if he were no longer there but had actually left a while ago, and what Pyotr was seeing now was merely his afterimage, a white imprint on the sky.

6

Black eyes

Istanbul, Turkey, 1955

The street, you said, was no place for a baby. At first my mother didn't listen; she kept me there. And you were wrong in any case. I was fine. You couldn't see it, but I was fine. I was wrapped up in her lap, I saw the world passing by, and when I liked it I looked at it and when I didn't I buried my head in her, in the folds of her rags and the sour milkiness of her bosom.

Later, when I had grown too big to be concealed in her garments, she could be persuaded. Scarcely had she unveiled me than I tumbled from her lap and into your home. I left her behind. How everything was transformed! From a shelter of fabric and flesh, and the cradle of her bony hands (she held me constantly, you know – even when one hand was outstretched, cupped, waiting for a coin to drop into it, the other was holding me tightly), to this vast, cool wooden house, through which shadows perpetually fell, and in which I first learnt to run. Such heavy steps at first. You must remember how, when you first brought me here, my little legs, so unaccustomed to interior space, thumped up and down the stairs and all through the various rooms and past their various things. Only later did I learn to become light; it was even a pleasure, sneaking around the place, avoiding the creaky floorboards. But it was a few years still before I was able to find my balance in your house – to be neither too heavy nor too light, and to move about it as though I belonged there.

That was the time of the occupation; the fighting was over and the Europeans had moved in. Of course, I had no knowledge of what was going on, no sense of the weight of those days. The troops in the street spoke strange languages and acted as if they owned the place, and I guess they did. I counted them lined up with their rifles, like toys. There were barriers and checkpoints, and submarines in the Bosphorus.

All this seemed quite normal to me as a young boy. Streets were places of instability, so what did it matter who was lording it over things? It did not concern me – not, at least, until those soldiers moved my mother on. You remember. You had taken me back to see her, as you did every so often, but she wasn't there. Not in her usual alcove in Boğazkesen Street, next to the brush shop. The soldiers, British I think, had been cleaning up their patch. But the patch was not clean, for there were many men out that day, protesting against the humiliation. This is one of my earliest memories – being carried on your shoulders above the throng in search of her. That day my mute shock and bewilderment found a voice in the emotions of the crowd, and when I recall it I almost feel again that churning fear that seemed to rise and sway from your body below. The fear that she had been engulfed somehow: by the crowd, by the city, by the forces of men whose sole purpose on earth was to shout, and against which my mother, so small and so quiet – I knew it even then – would never stand a chance. The fear that I would never see her again. That is why, I suppose, you thought you were rescuing me when you took me off the streets. You knew how easy it was for someone to disappear.

It was a miracle that we found her alive. That we passed through the mass and rounded the corner, into a new, weirdly empty street – and there she was. We approached, this tottering chimera of man and boy, and she looked up, past you to me, and as she tilted her head skywards her whole face was revealed. Her eyes widened, the pupils contracted in the light, but they were still dark, and at that moment I could feel the muscles in your neck tensing beneath me and I knew you were looking away from her. Gently you lowered me down and placed me beside her, and I crawled back into her folds, trying to find the space I had long since grown out of. But only for a little while. We couldn't stay long.

Ah, it's a lot to remember – a long way back. I hope my memory sharpens with age. Has yours, now that you are old? Do you remember that day more vividly than I? Perhaps you understand it better, at least. I have the feeling that I missed something, that everything happening below me was as if in a dream – logical, yet absurd – but then I also wonder if it is just that we always impose logic on events once they have passed.

You need water; forgive me, I should have noticed. Let me get you some. Here, your lips are very dry, wet them. Now speak if you can; try. If you cannot, no matter. Conserve your energy. You don't mind if I talk, though? Then I will continue, if I may.

Now that it has all come back to me, I need to order it somehow. Perhaps I am being too possessive of memories that are not exclusively mine; perhaps you suspect I am still just a selfish little boy. Ah, well. We all need something of our own, and all the more so in our youth, because it is from there that we gather the stuff for our future.

Blessed years. I had a happy childhood, if one is to judge a time by the predominant emotion of its recollection. I was the only boy in the house, the only child, and I cannot say that you treated me as anything other than your own. You took me to the Greek emporia and the sweet shops of Pera, sailing to Sariyer and swimming at Tarabya. We ate yogurt in Kanlıca and ice-cream in Ortaköy. Sometimes I visited you in the store, where you presided over reams and reams of fabric, remnants from the remnants of empire and of the world, and I had the impression – as I guess your customers did too – that you were some kind of sultan, perhaps the very last.

I wanted for nothing; you kept me safe. When, all of a sudden, fezzes vanished from the heads of men, and in their place thin-brimmed hats appeared, you made sure I would not feel left out, and had Nanny take me to be fitted with my own. When we went out together in our matching hats – such outings by then only rare, as you had become a businessman of some stature and, of course, I had my studies to think of – you did not correct people when they presumed me to be your son. Such a smart little boy like his father! And I too remained silent, for as far as I was concerned you were my father, for you were the only one I ever had.

It hurts – I can see. Have some more water, or is it time for your whisky? Indulge me a little longer and then I'll fetch you one. I promise.

Our country changed quickly after that. I saw it incrementally, each year on my birthday, when you took me back to my mother just as you had that day in the crowd. For an hour or so you left us alone together. I sat with her, looking not at her but at the world as she saw it. And then one day she vanished again. It was my eighth birthday that time. Oh, you told me not to worry, that she was not expecting us, that street folk knew nothing of what day it was, only the seasons. But I was born in October and the chestnuts had fallen, so she should have known to wait for me there. It remains with me still, the terrible shock and disappointment of arriving in the place where I expected to see her, and finding instead only a rag so eroded by the elements I could not even tell whether it belonged to her or not. You squeezed my hand encouragingly, led me around the corner to where she might also be, but she wasn't there either. We walked and walked and your hand gripped tighter around mine. And I can see now how even as we searched for her you tried to prepare me for the possibility of her death – 'My boy,' you shook your head, 'the streets are no place for a woman.' But you know I was still very young, and could not really comprehend.

I had become accustomed to my sheltered life with you, and it did not occur to me that my mother might become permanently lost – at least not to death. To the Byzantine streets, yes, that I could almost comprehend. For I saw her as a little stone that might have been dislodged and kicked into a corner...

But I digress. What I wanted to say was, it was an exciting time to grow up, in this new nation of ours. I grew up alongside it, and the expectations of each of us were great. You didn't let me forget that, did you? When my performance in my lessons was less than stellar, you scolded me. 'A fine citizen you will make! Would you have preferred that I left you on the streets?'

What a question! You always did throw me with that one. Would I have preferred to stay on the streets – illiterate, hungry, humiliated, but with her – or in your big house (grand, but not excessively so), well fed (to the point where I was even getting a bit chubby), with warmth and good friendships, a profession and a life laid out neatly before me, just as my school uniform was each morning?

You've caught me getting dewy-eyed. But do you see a single tear fall? No. You know me better than that. You know I would never weep in front of you. You may weep, though, if you wish. At your age, I think you are entitled. There it comes, a single tear – blink, you should blink, that will help it on its way – and I won't tell a soul. Get it all out, even if it is just that solitary tear, and then we can go on with our story. Here's your water. But I can tell by that look in your eyes, you would rather have a whisky. Very well, I have kept you waiting for it long enough.

I will just…shall I open the window? It's quiet out there tonight, so far at least. Not a whiff of smoke; a breeze has swept through. Oh dear, you're not looking at all well. I will open it, there. Now, back to that impossible question of yours…

The streets or your home, and which did I prefer. You thought you had made the decision for me, and that it was the right one. After my eighth birthday you stopped taking me to her. I suppose you thought it was time for me to grow up, to abandon that which was hopeless – that which did not attend to my future. You did not know, though, that I continued to look for her. Not only on my birthdays, but whenever I was free from the house. I patrolled the streets purposefully; I looked into the face of every woman I passed. Every man as well, in case his at least held some clue. The ice-cream and the egg sellers, the shoe shiners, the porters and the fishermen. The beggars, of course. Again and again, nothing. But to see all those people in the world, each defined against it, each unique – it only made me more determined. And it made me stronger.

I found her, too. Unbelievable, perhaps, but I had never imagined it wouldn't be so. It was several months later, and not so very far away from where I had last seen her. My mother could not explain to me why she had uprooted herself; she had very nearly stopped speaking altogether. But she did not move again, and later I took to seeing her every Friday afternoon, after my French lesson. Or during it, to be precise, since I struck a deal with Maître Lunel to be released half an hour before time. He was paid; I was making progress; everyone was happy; and you were none the wiser.

Don't be cross. I learnt more on the street than I could have in there. That's what you wanted, isn't it? To have an educated boy?

Those Fridays when I went to see my mother I sat beside her. Together we watched the world go by, like before. Absurd, isn't it? You can imagine how it looked! Me with my smart uniform and satchel, my teeth brushed and hair combed, plump and healthy, beside that bunch of rags and bones that was my mother. I'm not being cruel. I'm only saying how it must have looked to passers-by.

We talked a little or, that is to say, I talked. I told her about my life with you. I told her everything, without censorship and without giving a thought to what she might want to hear. She had a way of drawing things out of you, a kind of magnetism. But perhaps all mothers have that. She would squeeze my leg to continue. She never got bored.

I thrived on visiting her. You might imagine it was the subterfuge of it – though it's hardly the kind of boy's adventure of comic books! – or that it was simply that I loved and missed her, and yes, that is undoubtedly so. She was my mother. But I loved it also because it was the only time I could truly think. Being with her was a kind of solitude…not one that is filled with important and worthy thoughts, but one through which the world just flows. Her presence was a kind of absence, and one that I needed to make a space for myself.

She stank, of course. When it was time for me to say goodbye, when I leaned in to kiss her weathered face, half-hidden in the folds of her rags, I wondered how I could have lived in the cocoon of that smell for so long. I had to hold my breath to do it. At that moment it felt like the right time to leave.

It's a glorious evening – such a pity you can't see it from your corner of the room. Or perhaps you can? Ah, yes, but it's only a black triangle of sky, no stars or moon in it. I suppose you're wondering how the shop is doing in your absence. Very well, I can report. The Flemish linen is selling better than expected, and the demand for silk has not dropped – it's even gone up a little. The new boy has settled in and it's business as usual. Apart from – well, the front was a bit of a mess this morning, to be honest, after all the fuss last night. Some idiot smashed one of the display windows, and I had the boy sweep up the glass. What fuss? I can't believe you haven't heard about it. Mrs Başak didn't mention anything? Not wanting to trouble you, most likely. It was – how shall I put it – an incident with the Greeks. Some of our lot getting a little overenthusiastic. Burning and looting, that sort of thing. A few souls beaten. Killed? I don't know. Women, well, they were not spared. Disgraceful business. Terrible stuff. It'll do the trick, though – some of them have already gone. Anyway, your shop is all right.

I would fear for my mother if she were out there now, but she is not. She has a roof over her head, she has somewhere to retreat to. She is safe.

Yes, she is safe. She has been for a long time. I have been renting her a room, for several years now – I preferred you not to know. Nothing very salubrious, but a room nonetheless. Don't worry, it didn't come from your pocket. I had to do a little trading on the side, but I never stole a *kuruş,* only borrowed a little to start off with, and every bit of it I paid back. You never noticed, but I like to think that even if you had, you would at least have applauded my entrepreneurial spirit.

After I turned eight we never spoke of her again. Were you glad she had vanished? Such a pious woman, never showing her face to you, never removing her veil even for a second. Only her black eyes observing you. She scared you a little, I think – the superstition she represented, the inscrutability of her. Her stubborn unwillingness to speak, or to move from her spot, even as the city and history closed in on her. She was a force you did not quite know how to deal with. So I really do understand why you thought it best for me to forget her.

I myself tried, more than once, to have her remove her covering. At that time there was much talk of banning the veil; it seemed inevitable, and her persistence made me embarrassed for myself and for her. I was then just a young man, still so naive, for I imagined I could make my mother, a former beggar-woman, into a modern Turkish lady. I had seen peasant girls transform into flappers overnight, and fashionable White Russians stalking the streets with their make-up and cigarettes, and I imagined she could be rehabilitated too. I had given her a home, and to that she had added a little cleaning job, her own clothes and a few modest possessions. She had such potential! I harangued her from time to time, but she would not budge. Her head remained covered. God, it annoyed me! For many years I was almost angry about it. I wished she could be more forward-thinking, like you – more willing to move with the times. But then you cannot argue with someone who will not speak.

You look tired. I suppose I would be too, in your place. The moon is high, and I've been talking your head off. A drop more whisky? It should perk you up. Too much, though, will send you to sleep, and we don't want that. Best you stay awake for just a little longer. You might find it interesting.

Did you know, for instance, that my mother was always frightened of you? But then how could you not? She refused to look you in the eye; she recoiled when you approached. As a child I never noticed it. I guess I imagined her behaviour was simply that of a vulnerable woman with a powerful man, or any man. Even the one to whom you have entrusted your only child.

Now, you remember the day of my wedding. What a beautiful niece you had, and she is as beautiful now. Though I remember fondly the day Güldem and I joined our hearts together, I was glad when it was all over. My starched clothes and pomaded hair, my new wife made up almost beyond recognition, so that when I kissed her a powdery substance came off, as when one touches a moth. The expense of it all, which shamed me. And the absence of my mother, which you had long ago explained to the good people in your circle as a tragedy that accompanied my birth. After the ceremony I stole away and went to see her. Güldem knew, she understood; she wanted to come, but I asked her not to and she did not insist. She kept my secret. Alone I travelled across the water, to Üsküdar. At my mother's door I ran my fingers through my hair, dislodging the pomade. I loosened my cummerbund and with relief released my feet from those tight, expensive shoes.

She must have heard me kick them off, because immediately she appeared at the door, smiling, kissing me. She had been weeping; her eyes were still brimming with tears and she sniffled gently as I followed her into her quarters.

And then, right in front of me, my mother fell to the ground. Her body hit the floor with an almighty thud and began to curl and clench. Horrified, I approached her, called to her. Though her eyes were open, they were thrown back in her head, as if into some demonic realm. I tried first to hold her, then to shake her, but she seemed to be in the grip of a waking nightmare from which she could not be roused. For the longest time she twitched beneath me, unbreathing, as she took on a deathly pallor. I was sure she was approaching her end. And then as suddenly as it began it stopped, and slowly, groggily, she returned to herself – and to me.

In the course of this violence her veil had come loose, and by the time it was over it had dislodged completely. It was a sight I was not prepared for – that indeed no man would be. One side of her head was covered in thick black hair, flecked with silver; the other was a mess of tangled flesh and scar tissue. On that side the curve of her head seemed to fall away, as though it had been caved in, then picked at by scavengers seeking vulnerable flesh.

When she returned to her senses I asked her what had happened, and who had done this to her. She sucked at her injured tongue, which she had bitten at fiercely, and looked at me with sorrow. As I waited for her to find the words I realised that this was not a new injury, for the scar tissue had long since healed and hardened, but one that had been inflicted some time ago. My mother had spent many years concealing her mutilation from me, and from the world.

I had always known she wasn't from here, but I had never guessed from just how far she had come. In a small voice that did not conceal her poor command of the Turkish language, nor reveal anything else, she finally told me her story. How she had been born in the far east, in a town of Christians and Jews, and of her Assyrian kin. I see you understand now as I did then: a village of Syriacs, Jews and Armenians on the eve of the Great War – to call it doomed would have been optimistic. In the massacres she lost everything. She was brutalised unspeakably, struck down with her wounds. She slipped in and out of consciousness, dragged herself off to die. Only by the grace of God did she not. And only by the grace of a herder's family, who took her in, did she begin to restore herself to life.

When she had found strength enough she embarked on her journey here. She might have found refuge closer by, in the Syrian lands, but her family were in Istanbul – her rich cousins from the West. She had never met them, but she knew that they owned a business on Boğazkesen, and she knew that they would take her in. Here she would start a new life. My mother had always dreamt of coming to the city. What youth from a dusty town does not? She did not understand that she was travelling to the very place from which the plan to exterminate her people had come.

But they were not there, her people. Yes, and now you see my point. When did your family acquire the shop on Boğazkesen? And when did you first see her, dishevelled, stooping, wandering in confusion up and down the street? You must have, because she did it for weeks, examining every single shop, approaching each one. Though she could not read she remembered the shape of the numbers from the envelopes sent by her rich cousins from the West, the double cross of two fours. The numbers she saw mirrored in the gold paint above your door.

She dragged herself back and forth up that street, until one day she stopped and sat down – right in that spot where I spent my first years, only a few metres from your doorstep, from which she could observe every customer enter and leave, and from which you could see her too. She cannot be entirely certain that it is your store that once belonged to her family, but she knows it nevertheless. And so, I think, do you.

Her one certainty in life was the coin that you would drop into her hand every day. You knew she was not a pious follower of Allah, but both of you allowed the gentle lie to stand. When I was born (of a shameful conception, but don't worry, I know you had no hand in it), you knew what you had to do. You watched me struggle, sickly, at her breast, then offered to take me in. You ground her down with your reasoning and your insistence, and in the end she allowed you to take me as your own.

Now, is that a look of incredulity in your old, bleary eyes? Perhaps you doubt my story. After all, these seizures sound improbable, for in all that time she spent outside your shop you never saw her suffer one. Well, do you know, neither did I. It was not until after she had left the streets that they began. Funny, how those spasms demanded a kind of privacy that even childbirth had not. I have in fact consulted with some physicians about this. One of them, a disciple of Dr Freud, suggested that it was a psychological disturbance triggered by some kind of infantile trauma. I had explained to him that the injuries on her head were the result of being attacked by a dog in her youth – this story delighted him, and from this he proposed the explanation that the seizures probably only occurred when, as an adult, she spied a dog in the street. I cannot blame the man for his ignorance, of course, since it was I who had fed him the dog story – not a good base for a sound diagnosis, but then I could hardly tell him the truth, could I?

The other two proposed a physiological trauma (*trauma!* It must be the fashion of today – how I tire of hearing the word), the delayed onset of grand mal seizures due to damage to the cerebral cortex – if you'll forgive the technical language. One of these experts recommended shock treatment, the other unhesitatingly prescribed pharmaceuticals. I am not sure what I think, but my mother, who refuses to let anyone but me touch her, knows only that she would not be as she is if she had been allowed to lead a peaceful life.

The other day it occurred to me – should I take her to mass? Do you know that for all those years she lived less than a thousand yards from the Assyrian Church, without ever going in? And here she was, posing as one of Allah's faithful to all who passed! Not that she intended to deceive. She only wanted to cover her shame. If she had known the church was there, perhaps she would have gone in. Perhaps she would have taken me in there too. Perhaps it would have saved us. Anyway, it is too late for all that.

You seem to be listening to me still, but I cannot be sure. Doesn't your head feel heavy? That is the whisky – you were never one to resist a drop. Don't you feel as if you were about to die? That is the barbiturate. Mother's prescription, but she refuses to take it, and I don't want it going to waste. Your illness has been too long now, and I have become impatient. A ship sails to France next week. Before that I need to sell the store, put all our affairs in order. I imagined you would die long ago, and then we could leave. But you haven't, so you must forgive me for hurrying things along. There is much to do and so little time to do it.

I have to credit those hooligans the other night for the idea. Oh, I do not mean that it was a decision made in haste, only that until then it had not occurred to me what precisely must be done. That if you are no longer here, perhaps this house ought not to be either. There is a chance, of course, that the flames will leap – this old city burns so easily. But it is a still night, and it is really only this room that I want erased. Don't be afraid. The barbiturate is working, and not until you have fallen asleep will the lamp topple from your bedside and gather you up in flames. Perhaps you are already asleep, and I have been talking to myself all this time. I may have miscalculated the dosage. But what do I know about medicine? I am educated, but not so much as that.

And do not worry about Güldem, or the twins. They are coming with me. Mother, too. It is true that when this house begins to smoulder, and I have ushered everyone safely out into the street, that they will no longer have anywhere to live. But God willing we will be on that ship soon, and it will not be long before we find a home once more. For the streets are no place for a woman, or a child.

7

Visitor from Hollywood

Łódź, Poland, 1966

And now you check they're all even, Wiesława says. She has taken the heavy pan from her granddaughter and poured the remainder of the hot syrup into the last two jars, on an angle so as to avoid splashing any. This is precisely the same lesson she has been giving Ewa for the last fifteen years, but it doesn't hurt to do it again, so they bob down, the two of them, and survey the four jars of pale yellow *kompot* lined up on the kitchen bench. As Wiesława expected, the dried apple pieces are not evenly distributed, but Ewa has a good excuse for not getting it right – it's hard enough lifting the pan with one hand, let alone spreading everything out evenly. And it's not the end of the world, a spoon will sort out the apples. Ewa can manage that at least, and when it's done Wiesława takes the jars over to cool by the window, and says, Where on earth is Monika, she's taking her sweet time!

Monika is her other granddaughter, she's twenty-three, a little older than Ewa. Wiesława's sent her to get some water from the neighbours downstairs, once again the water hasn't quite managed to make it up to their floor, all they get is a strained gurgling in the pipes. It's a bother, but life doesn't stop just because the water does, somebody else will have some. Now they've made the *kompot* there's no water left for a pot of tea, or anything else for that matter. Why did she send Monika, who can't be relied on to hurry back, well, she sent her because Monika shows absolutely no interest in cooking, running around is more her thing, which is all very well and good but she has to run back again too!

When Monika finally gets in Wiesława is ready with her red hands on her hips and her usual, So where did you get to, Warsaw? I hope you gave my regards to the Cardinal! And Monika puts down the canister, puffing, explaining that she had to knock around, there's no water on the third either, but eventually Mrs Królikowska was home, she helped out. Huh, Wiesława says, didn't I tell you not to ask that lot for favours, who knows what they'll want in return? You wanted water didn't you, Monika cries, she still hasn't got her breath back, I've got a run in my stocking now going up and down all those damned stairs so a bit of gratitude would be nice! But Ewa is grateful, Thank you, Niczka, she says, that's what she calls her older sister, and she tries to take the water from her to put in the kettle but she's having trouble managing it, it's pretty heavy, so Monika goes over, Careful now love, give me that side, and together they take it over to the stove and Monika holds the canister steady with her two hands while Ewa scoops in the water with her one. Not too much! Wiesława calls out behind them, she can't help but oversee proceedings, what with one granddaughter who's a cripple and the other who's not exactly the homemaking type. From the back they look more or less the same, except that Monika is a little taller, that's entirely normal, and you wouldn't even know that there was anything wrong with Ewa. It's true that Monika has a run in her stocking, a big one at the back of her knee, but Wiesława isn't sure that it was going up and down the stairs that put it there, more likely she got it running around with boys. You wouldn't know anything was wrong with Monika either, from the back. She looks so responsible and dedicated, standing there helping her poor little sister with the tea.

Four-thirty is the hour they awake; there's one little alarm clock that rouses them all. Wiesława goes to one factory, Ewa to another, and Monika heads off to the bakery. Ewa leaves the flat a bit later than the other two, however – they don't start so early at the War Invalids factory for some reason, perhaps it's a kindness. Nevertheless Ewa doesn't sleep in even though she can, it's better that they all have the same routine, seeing as they're sharing a room, the household functions better that way. Though that doesn't stop Monika getting in late some nights, sometimes she's so late the other two are already in bed and then she disturbs them coming in, there's no way they can't hear the sound of the key in the lock, the clunk of her bag on the ground or the rustle of her changing out of her clothes, even the sound of her stockings coming off slithers towards them. How does she have the energy to stay up so late, Wiesława wonders, maybe because she doesn't work that hard, after all she's just a shop girl handing out loaves all day, she isn't even baking the stuff, it's not the most strenuous job in the world.

Cucumber's coming, someone says, that's what the buses are called around here on account of their shape, though Wiesława can't see it, what a silly name, if they were cucumbers they would at least be painted green and not white as they are. The bus sighs when it pulls up and she sighs when she gets in. Wiesława sighs a lot – someone pointed this out to her once – which leads her to wonder if she isn't exhaling more than she is inhaling, that's a bit of a silly idea too, but then she isn't one of those tubby *babcie* who look as though they've been inflated, she's actually quite thin, although it wouldn't be right to say she'd kept her figure either, because she definitely is not the same shape as she once was, things have moved around a bit since she was young.

By the time she arrives at the factory gate the sky is filled with light, the best time of the day because it's clearest now, even though the chimneys have been smouldering away overnight (this city of chimneys never entirely shuts down), but it's just a fine film of smoke, it doesn't get in the way of a beautiful sunrise. And it's just as well Wiesława can enjoy it now, since she'll be inside all day, though at least it's summer and it'll be light outside when she leaves too. The worst is in winter, when she lives in perpetual night – she exits the factory and there is only a scrap of the day left, and everybody is rushing home as the darkness falls in clumps around them.

At her station there is a logical sequence of duties to be performed: coat to be buttoned up, dust to be cleared, floor to be swept, threads to be spooled, switches to be thrown, et cetera, and in just the same way Wiesława entertains a sequence of thoughts, in more or less the same logical order, every day. She begins quite alert, concentrating on her work, and this is how it should be, the machines can be quite dangerous if you lose sight of what you're doing. They already have one person with a mangled hand in the house, they don't need another. About an hour later though her concentration lapses, making way for the thought that her feet hurt, but she won't be able to sit down for a while longer, so she'll have to put up with it. This thought is directly followed by one that her knees are aching now too. And her arms as well, because there's an awful lot of reaching up and pulling involved here, restringing the machine when there's a jam and so forth, and from there the next thought is inevitable – her whole body is aching. Wiesława is about to issue a private condemnation of the factory when she's forced to concede to herself that her whole body used to ache in the village too, but, she swiftly counters, also to herself, *that* was different, back then she had a certain amount of control over her work, she could sit down if she wanted, there was a bit more variety, here it's just the same thing over and over. No wind coming to greet her, no sun bristling her skin, no hay or dirt or animal smells, only those of grease and warm fabric...And no colour and no light, at least not the right kind. By now you'd think she'd be used to this, a third of her life she's been here, but it's not the case. Once a peasant always a peasant, a neighbour said to her one time, the woman had meant it as an insult but it's true, it can't be denied, and there's no shame in it.

It was only the war that had pushed and prodded them out of the village – it had herded them like animals, far from home. But the decision not to return had been theirs, they came to the city instead. The girls had lost their parents, Wiesława's son and his wife, who died two years apart of different causes but the result was the same, that is that the girls needed someone to take care of them, and especially Ewa, not everyone would survive a thing like that. Thank God she'd only been little and didn't remember any of it. It was Wiesława's husband Krzysztof's idea, to make a new start away from the wreckage, but as it turned out he didn't last long either. He only stayed by her side another five years and then he dropped dead on her too, obviously city life didn't agree with him either. But she'd long ago stopped being angry with him about that, so his death wasn't part of the sequence of her thoughts any more. Krzysztof was there, but only as a trace of sadness beneath the surface, part of the general mood of regret that usually came over her at about this point in the day.

At the time it seemed like a good idea, Łódź was still standing, unlike Warsaw, or the rest of Europe, it seemed a blessed place somehow. And to be fair she wanted to move at first, Wiesława did, after losing her son she'd been ready for a change of scene. Now though the only one who is profiting from this move is Monika, who came to the city like a knife to butter, that is to say, she isn't interested in staying at home and helping out there, she prefers to go out with her friends from the Film School, that's where the cool girls hang out, that's the place to be, that's where it's at, jazz music and cigarettes, it's the real scene – Monika says. And if she isn't there then she's at the Honoratka with her pals, drinking neon pink and eating apple cake, or in the restaurant across the road boozing it up, or gossiping in the toilets of the Grand Hotel, and if she isn't there then Wiesława doesn't want to know, on the streets somewhere, not to say that Monika's a street girl, no, Wiesława doesn't think her granddaughter is that, but then she does have more money than she, a shop girl, ought to, who can say, perhaps her admirers buy her things, that's how it is for pretty girls and that's how it always will be. Ewa is pretty too but her stump of a hand really ruins things, though perhaps this isn't the worst fate for a girl – Ewa might have trouble finding a husband but it's Monika who's on a more dangerous path, Monika still doesn't have a steady boyfriend, if she keeps going like this she'll end up an old maid, or get herself knocked up, in fact it's a wonder that hasn't happened already, and then who do you suppose will be looking after the baby? The neighbours call her *latawica*, hussy, whether this is because they know something Wiesława doesn't she can't say, but in any case, with Monika staying out late all the time she can't defend her, so when someone mutters the word what can she do? She can pretend not to hear, that's all.

And, who knows, perhaps Monika will be all right, perhaps she'll meet a famous actor or director, this is the hope of all the girls in the Film School crowd. Perhaps life will be okay for her. This week is a big deal, an American actor is coming to the school, Kirk Douglas is his name, everybody knows who he is and if they don't it's enough to say, You know, the one with the dimple, and he is a striking-looking man, no one can quite believe it, that *he* would come *here*. Monika's been going on about it for ages, perhaps he's the one she's got her sights on, she's aiming high, but that's our Monika. Yes, Monika is the only one who has profited from city life.

It's harder for Ewa, she's a sentimental soul, a bit of a daydreamer. That's no help for a factory girl, but what else can she do? The Institute is there just for people like her, otherwise she'd have nothing, and anything is better than nothing. She makes wooden toys in there, someone has to do it, sometimes she brings the factory seconds home, gives them out to the kids in the neighbourhood and then later you see them playing with them in the dirt, the wood turning as black as their feet, but they're happy. The young kids like Ewa but then they grow up a bit and they learn to be cruel. The thing that hurts her most is when they sing 'Little Cuckoo' at her: '*Kukułeczka kuka*, the cuckoo bird is cuckooing, a young man is looking for a girl, cuc-koo, cuc-koo...,' this is what the kids do ever since they discovered it was her grandmother's pet name for her, on account of the lottery forms she used to bring home – Little Cuckoo forms, they give them out at the Institute, not that Wiesława would ever play the lottery, gambling is not only a sin, it's a foolish waste. Wiesława only started calling her *Kukułeczka* to gently tease her, but then the local brats started it too and they do it to be mean. Ewa hasn't got a boyfriend, it hurts her terribly, so she doesn't bring the tickets anymore, not even for her sister, and nobody utters the word at home, *Kukułeczka*, such a pity because it really does suit her and Wiesława stills thinks of Ewa as her little cuckoo – her little injured bird.

The thing Wiesława likes most is to go out Sunday mushrooming with Ewa, it's probably the girl's favourite thing too, they go to the woods together and spend hours and hours walking in a trance over the lush, mossy ground, each of them has a basket and by the end of the day the baskets are full. Then they come home and dry or pickle half of them, and the rest they eat straight away. Monika never comes mushrooming with them but she doesn't mind eating the proceeds, it's been so long for her she couldn't even be trusted to pick the good ones, whereas Ewa has the knack, her eyes are trained and even with her bad hand she twists and pulls the stalks just right. She takes care with what she does. Wiesława often has the thought, when she sees Ewa with her basket over one arm, cradling the newly picked mushrooms, that she'd be a good mother, the only problem is she's too devoted, that's her weakness, she's sentimental and devoted, like when the dog that hung around at the foot of the stairwell died suddenly and she sobbed over it for days. That's the thing, you can't be so attached to animals, nor can you really afford to be with humans, although that's much more of a challenge, Wiesława will admit. Anyway, this kind of thing sometimes makes her think twice about whether Ewa is cut out for village life after all. You see Wiesława has long entertained the thought of abandoning the city and going back there, taking Ewa with her, it's not a very likely prospect but this is something she thinks about. In that sequence of everyday thoughts it slots in very nicely.

Of course, this is dangerous thinking. Going back to the village, does she really think they'd be allowed to leave so easily? That's what Monika said the first time Wiesława brought it up a year or so ago, Wouldn't it be nice if we could all go back and live in the village again? and Monika had laughed, Don't be ridiculous, should we all pick turnips for the rest of our days? Monika has decided her fate, but Ewa's is still open. Maybe that's for the best, maybe not, Wiesława's greatest worry is that it will be the young one who gets herself up the duff first – she's not convinced that sentimental Ewa wouldn't sleep with a man just because he looked at her with his sad, doggy eyes, in that craven way men sometimes do when they've had a few and they're wallowing in self-pity, and there happens to be a woman there to listen to them. In Ewa's case they'd probably take one look at her and say to themselves, Now, this one shouldn't be too hard, she's as pathetic as me and twice as kind, and Wiesława can imagine that the first one of these men Ewa meets will seal her fate, so maybe she's better off with just dogs and pot plants to care for, unless she finds a good village boy, which is the ideal scenario, and it's not too late for that.

This is the sequence of thoughts, always: her aches, and Monika and Ewa, at the end coming back round to her pain again, dear God her knees are killing her, especially the right one, she's not getting any younger, but at least it's nearly break time, thank God.

After work Wiesława never knows what she is going to do until the last minute, whether she will catch the bus or walk home. It's not much for the bus but money is money, it could be used for other things, sometimes she likes to save those *grosze*. The only question is whether her legs will take it. So each day she goes to the bus stop with the rest of the workers and then either her pains will win out and she'll stay there, standing in the line with the rest of them, or she'll keep walking, propelled by the idea of those coins she'll save, or the nice weather or simply not wanting to be shut up in a bus, she's had enough of that, she's someone who needs a bit of space. Today she's walking, and although today she had the same thoughts as she has every other day, they weigh heavier upon her, they crowd her, the claustrophobic feeling is overwhelming, there was really no chance of her getting on that bus today to be crowded further. The streets are bustling but the sky, those gentle colours, the smoke, the serene folding into dusk, she might get wrapped up in it too, that weary sky, she just has to watch where she's going. She follows the ribbon of light as it unfurls to her home, sighs but does not pause, and climbing the stairs makes no attempt to calm her breath, four floors up and the gap between the steps is enormous, they say whoever designed it was a giant, a sadist or a fool, you really have to haul yourself up each one. Her puffing as she passes the third floor landing is so loud, it's the cue for Ewa to warm dinner up, sometimes they eat together but sometimes Ewa needs to start before her *babcia* gets home, who can blame her, she too works hard all day, just because they're invalids in there doesn't mean they have it easy. Monika isn't home tonight, she'll eat when she gets in, who knows when that's going to be, so Wiesława and Ewa set aside a portion for her and she'll have it later, but hopefully not too late, it's no fun trying to sleep when you can hear a spoon scraping against a pan.

Wiesława and Ewa have dinner in silence, they're both tired but Ewa is upset about something too. She's been crying but won't say what about, she just sits there sniffling and wiping her face with her hand – the good one of course, the bad one is buried in her lap like always. She's trying to eat but her spoon is shaking and it's clear her unhappiness is choking her up, perhaps she was bullied today. Is this what we came here for? Wiesława asks herself, not for the first time, and again she thinks they would have been better off staying where they were, a clean life where folk respect each other, they'd be poorer but happier. Perhaps it's not such a crazy idea, it's a hard life but no harder than this, it's not like things are going to get better here, if anything they'll get worse. Perhaps she'll mention it to Ewa one day, but now's not right, so in the meantime she'll keep thinking about it and saving her bus fare, just in case. As for Monika, she won't want to come, her life is in Łódź, she'd only laugh and ridicule them, there's no point in mentioning it to her.

Once in a while Wiesława pays a visit to the village, it takes her nearly half a day to get there and apart from in the summer holidays she can't stay long, usually it's just a few hours and then she has to travel all the way back again. These short visits are only just enough to sustain her – the smell of the hay, the low murmur of the cows, her sister-in-law's deer sausages, other folks' children, who mature in her absence – these keep both her hope and her despair alive. There, she knows she is in her place. And that's strange, because actually it's not her village, it's her late husband's, her village is just few miles away but she doesn't go there any more, they don't really get on. Krzysztof's family is more hers, they are the ones who have always welcomed her, and that means more somehow, because by choosing him she chose them. They appreciate that, they accept her. They always did what they could to help make a home for her and her sons, of which there'd been three: baby Tadeusz who died in infancy; Olek, who survived the war but went to Wrocław; and Maciek, the girls' father, who didn't. Wiesława thought that after they moved to Łódź and her husband died that would be it, the tie would be broken, after all they'd abandoned his village at the war's end, it wasn't good form but they weren't the only ones to do that. But no, his family didn't hold a grudge, perhaps they understood how at the time it had seemed like the best hope for the girls, and Ewa especially. And maybe it was back then – the best hope – but she's not a child any more, times change, and a good decision made one day doesn't necessarily stay one forever.

They welcome her, they tell her she should move back, perhaps it's just talk, just hospitality, but this is how it always goes, they've mentioned it more than once – there are houses lying vacant and isn't she sick of being cooped up in a factory all day? She's not a chicken after all! Don't get me started, Wiesława will say, and everyone laughs, convinced that their life, for all its hardships, is the best one possible. At least that's how it seems on a Sunday afternoon, with everyone so full and tipsy, and then she has to get back on the bus again, leaving everything behind, while her in-laws go and sleep off the meal, and the cows keep on their murmuring to the world.

This is the thought that comes to Wiesława the next day, and she's sure that if she moved back to the village she would never leave it again, not ever. Even if they threatened to arrest her, even if she didn't get her pension. She would take Ewa with her and Monika would visit, if she could be bothered. There's not a single thing Wiesława would miss about Łódź, except the picture houses, which she sometimes goes to on her day off, not that she's been for a while, and the trams, which seem to her gentle, elegant, noble and strong – like horses, but of course in the village there are real horses, so if she was there she wouldn't need the trams any more.

It gives her a kind of energy, this melding of past and future. Her body's still aching but now it seems to ache towards a purpose, and now when she leaves work she strides past the bus stop and the people queuing there, today there's no deliberation, she cannot not walk, and the energy lasts until she's in at the foot of the stairs and then it hits her, she's dog tired. At the first floor she's already wheezing with the effort, she overdid it a bit, she walked a bit too fast, but she had to hurry home, for today's the day she'll tell Ewa her plans. Yes, today's the day. At the door is the smell of a meal cooked, stuffed cabbage rolls, her favourite. She casts off her bag and goes into the kitchen, expecting to find Ewa in there. Nobody. The cabbage rolls are sitting in a dish, they've gone cold, the fat waxy around them. The apartment is empty. There's a loaf of bread on the bench, this means Monika has also come and gone, for she always brings a loaf home after work, and this time there's a poppyseed bun there too. Under the sugar jar nearby is a note, *Dear Babcia, I have gone out with Niczka, hope that's okay, love Ewa,* and beneath it Monika's scrawl, *I have stolen her for the evening! Don't worry. M. (The bun is for you!)* As if a bun will make everything all right, it's not even fresh, neither is the bread in fact. They're both from this morning, which means Monika hasn't just come home and gone out again after all. And since the cabbage rolls are stone cold too, she knows Ewa's been out for several hours as well, the sisters have been out together all day, they've taken the day off, both of them. And Wiesława knows why. It's that American actor, the one with the dimple, she knew it was this week he was coming but not the day, even though everyone's been talking about it for ages, Monika in particular has really been going on about it. So, she's dragged her little sister along to hang around the Film School with the other girls, and some of those girls will be real hussies, trying to catch a glimpse of the star, hoping he'll catch a glimpse of her and maybe take a liking to her and take her home – to America that is. Wiesława doesn't know if Mr Douglas is married already but that might not be a problem, Americans marry as often as Christmas, even if he is he might replace her with a Polish bride, that's if they let the lucky girl out of the country, you never know. She imagines Monika will be wearing her pink dress and red scarf – this is her attention-seeking outfit, for when she wants to impress – and as she goes through Monika's things to check what's missing she has the satisfaction of seeing she is right. Ewa will be wearing her only going-out outfit, but quite likely Monika has dolled her up for the occasion too, it wouldn't be the first time she's encouraged Ewa to improve herself. From time to time Wiesława has caught Ewa with traces of rouge and lipstick, they're just girls playing at dress-ups when it comes down to it. Still, Monika being the older one she should know better, what will it be like for Ewa when, if she ever does get to meet her idol, he notices her horrible stump? He'll flinch, that's what people do, even if they're trying to be nice, and that won't do Ewa any good, poor thing, to be rejected by someone like that, an American of all people, being teased or pitied by everyday folks is one thing, but when it comes to a Hollywood star you'd want to hold on to your illusions – any girl would – that you're in with a chance, even if it is very remote, that by some miracle or accident of fate it might be possible that he sees what is special in you, that he chooses *you*. Well with Ewa there's no chance at all, not a shred, Monika can do what she likes but she should have known better than to drag her little sister along and give her false hope.

Wiesława prepares some tea, nibbles on a slice of the poppyseed bun, she's breaking her own rule never to eat treats before a meal but she won't touch the cabbage rolls yet, she'll wait for Ewa to come in. She can picture her with her crushed hand behind her back, while with the other she offers Mr Dimple a posy of flowers that she's picked off the roadside. Poor thing, she's never had a man pay her the slightest bit of attention, not counting that time when it looked like one of the neighbour's boys was a bit sweet on her, but that was never going to go anywhere, and it didn't, either.

Time passes, Wiesława is still sitting there, and then at some point in the night she realises it's coming to an end, the blue day is sifting in. She's stayed up all night and still Ewa and Monika aren't back. That's not a good sign, she thinks, that means they're too ashamed to show their faces. Oh God, hopefully Ewa hasn't gone and done anything stupid, why didn't she take her off to the village before things got to this point, why did she wait so long? Most likely Monika will stagger in at dawn and then be straight off to work, if she's able, but Ewa will stay a bit to face the music. Poor little cuckoo, she'll be terrified, she'll expect to be punished. But there's no point in that, she'll never do anything like this again, and Kirk Douglas won't be returning to Łódź, why would he? Suddenly Wiesława feels incredibly tired and she realises that it'll soon be the time when she has to prepare herself for a working day too, yet she can't, she can't go out until Ewa gets back. So she just sits and waits a bit longer, until the sun is higher in the sky and the moment has passed when she might have any chance of getting to work on time. The dawn is beautiful, she doesn't often observe it at leisure like this, although once as a young bride she and Krzysztof would go together at first light, before the chores began, just to be together watching the sun come up, it only lasts a minute but it seemed longer back then. Wiesława sits a while more and then it is past the time when she won't get a severe reprimand, but still she can't leave because Ewa's not home yet, so that's suddenly that – she's had her last day in the factory, she didn't exactly plan it like this but there you go, the decision's made. In she goes to the bedroom and begins packing her belongings, and when that's done she packs Ewa's too, not everything, just the basics, Monika will come and bring them the rest later, and besides everything they really need is in the village already. Wiesława counts out the coins in her tin, money that she's saved by not taking the bus. It's enough to get them both back there and take a little gift to the in-laws also, you can't turn up empty-handed, and she'll need their help after all. Her stomach is growling, it's hours now since she ate that bun, so she goes to the stove and lights the flame under the cabbage rolls. She was going to wait till Ewa got home, but it's got to be any minute now, and it'll be much nicer for the girl to come in to a warm meal. Then Ewa will see that everything is okay, that she's not in trouble, and they'll eat together and then, when they're done, it will be just about time to leave. Wiesława stands there listening to the hiss of the flame under the dish, it's bubbling now, and for the puffing noises at the top of the stairs that will tell her Ewa is home.

8

Tiflis papers

Dagestan Oblast, Russian Empire, 1909

In the late winter of 1907, Alexander Aitken, twenty-two, a native of Fife and latterly educated at the University in Edinburgh, travelled from Scotland to Tiflis at the expense of the British Gramophone Company, which had hired him for his engineering expertise (acquired through his studies and his father, also an engineer) and his linguistic competencies (he had mastered Persian, Ancient Greek, Latin, French and German), to traverse the Russian Empire in what were to be its final years, and to record — for posterity and profit — the musical heritage of that vast and varied land. Aitken was tasked with visiting as many places as possible before the emissaries of the rival Pathé Company staked their claim. His first journey was a success — after arriving at his employer's office in Tiflis, and armed with his recording equipment and a Russian phrasebook, Aitken spent several months traversing the Caucasus and returned with a fine collection of songs. He labelled and catalogued the music, then set out again, similarly prepared — although his Russian was by now much advanced and he no longer had any need of the phrasebook. This time he was to

go further afield, to Vladikavkaz, Petrovsk-Port, Baku, Tabriz,
Rasht, Tehran and those isolated realms in between. From this
second mission, however, Alexander Aitken never returned. These
notes, made by Aitken himself, are all that remain.

I

The mountain passage was not any easier the second time.
The roads and paths are quite ruined by months of rain, and
my former guide was impossible to find, so I was saddled
instead with a young fellow, still just a boy, with bright blue
eyes and coppery wisps on his chin, who only took me as
far as Kazbegi. I wondered if he might be Circassian, or
what peculiar mix of mountain tribes he had come from.
The journey did not start out well – my horse seemed to be
of bad temper, shaking its head and snorting constantly, but
I soon realised that it had simply been bridled poorly, and
it was the chafing of metal that caused its irritation. We
stopped and the surly adolescent fixed his error. Yet the
re-bridled beast was no more cooperative, and my attempts
to whip him into action proved futile, so that eventually my
guide had to harness my horse to his own and lead me on a
rope through the mountains. This embarrassed us both. At
Kazbegi I slept and changed guides, but this one, though
older, was not much wiser, and his horses in even worse
condition. It took the longest time for our party to traverse
the mountains. Finally we reached Temir-Khan-Shura, a
sorry little town of mud and mosquitoes. I thanked him and
paid him well, but he refused to take me the extra distance
to the *aul* that was my destination, so I had to find a local to
do it. The sight of the two men transferring my equipment

as though it were a newly slaughtered animal was enough to jolt me out of the reverie the silence and the mountains had inspired. '*Hye-tcho!*' I cried out, before issuing a rebuke in Russian. I have learnt that the first interjection must always be in the local language, which mollifies them before I then give an order in the master's tongue. If I start with Russian I get nowhere.

Once on that final stage of the journey my reverie returned to me. I had been chatting a while with the new guide, a silkworm farmer whose wife had recently passed away bearing their eleventh child, but as soon as we exhausted our dialogue the great mountains crowded back in. I had forgotten what they were like, how in their vastness they open up a space for contemplation that is almost frightening in its breadth. No wonder the folk here are so godly, whatever their faith – they have nowhere to hide from the heavens. And the green, as vivid as anything I have seen back home, but more vital somehow, for it descends from the mist like something perpetually born.

By the time we arrived it was late, well after dark. At first the path had been familiar to me – I traced in the swaying and lunging of my horse the rocky outcrop surrounding the *aul*, and I felt a sense of tipsy homecoming, for though I have only been here once before, I knew I would be welcomed. Yet as the light faded and the half-obscured moonlight cast only gauzy shadows, my certainty vanished, and I began to wonder if the guide was taking me to the right village after all – if he hadn't decided to change course halfway, and hand me and my equipment over to bandits under the cover of night. But no, he was honourable – as is every other man I have encountered here. He took me, as I had asked, to Hamid's door. The tread of our horses was met by footsteps on the other side of it. What a sight for weary travellers – Hamid's wife, Aminat, standing silhouetted against the warmth of their home, waiting for us to come in.

2

It is true that men who do not live like others do not keep the same time as them. When I arrived late the other night my host was wide awake, eager to talk with me. He was occupying precisely the same spot on the same felted mat as when I had left him two years earlier, and he sat sternly as we waited for Aminat to finish laying out our food. Hamid and the guide performed their prayers, and an ablutionary – I suppose – sweeping down across the face, and the guide and I began to eat under the eye of our host. He did not touch the offerings, a simple but excellent meal of flatbread, honey, sticky white cheese and a type of green onion. When the guide had finished he stood and left. He had refused Hamid's offer to stay as a guest the night – I imagine he wanted to return to his many children. We heard him riding off again, beginning the long journey back in the dark, and when the last trace of him was gone Hamid began to warm and loosen, like cold hands over a fire.

'Welcome back, my friend,' he said, smiling broadly. 'I wonder if you remembered to bring something to toast our re-acquaintance?'

I had not forgotten – how could I? His last words to me, when I was taking my leave those two years ago, were these: 'God willing you will not return empty-handed, and as I offer you everything I have, in the spirit of godly brotherhood, may you do the same. May our friendship be one of mutual benefit, as the best are, united against enemies, in the service of joy, which might blossom for each man and his sons.' By all this he meant that if I returned I was to bring him vodka, which he stated explicitly only later, when he pulled me aside to clarify the terms of our warm new friendship. He had dared not ask for it directly in the company of others, for its consumption is forbidden in the *aul*. The inhabitants of this small township are devout – they follow the example of Hadji Zurab, its self-appointed leader, who frowns upon intoxicants. And so poor Hamid has to rely on a vanishing network of discreet and sympathetic outsiders, such as I, to furnish his vice.

Thus from my bag I produced a bottle of the liquor, one of several I had purchased in Tiflis at the outset of the journey. 'Is that all?' my host asked, a look of dismay clouding his face. I told him it was not, but reminded him that my equipment was heavy too, and the value of our friendship could not be measured by the quantity of drink I had brought, since my generosity was limited by the strength of the beasts that ferried my load. 'Ah yes, your equipment,' he replied. 'Tonight we will drink, and tomorrow you will get your music. I have something extra special for you, something new – you will be delighted.' He poured me a glass and I drank it all at once, but through weariness rather than deference to custom, for I was anxious to lay my head down, and expected he would not dismiss me until I had toasted with him. Yet Hamid relinquished my company easily, bidding me goodnight without further declarations, and in the morning I saw why – the bottle I had brought him was empty, as I discovered when I went to put on my boot and found it standing inside, hidden there. My host, it seemed, had been happy to consume the rest all by himself.

He did not rouse until after noon. I breakfasted, with Aminat bustling around me in her bonny charivari trousers, which are plump and swollen at the ankles, so that she resembles a ripe fruit swaying on the branch. I then busied myself by preparing my equipment for our recording session and, when that was done, walked around the *aul*, re-acquainting myself with its nooks and nodding good day to its inhabitants. Those who have not seen me before regard me with evident curiosity. I am not a local, nor a Russian. Rather, I am like a strange beast that nobody quite knows what to do with...Train it? Kill and eat it? Flee from it? Unsure, they keep their wary distance and I, wishing to retain mine, am sparing with my greetings.

And yet I am glad to be here. In truth, I needn't be. I recorded a great deal of this region's offerings on my last excursion. I recorded Hamid's music then, too. So I ought to be moving on to uncharted places. But Hamid asked me to come back, and though his motives may not be ones of pure hospitality, I was compelled to accept. I have entertained thoughts of my return from the moment I left.

3

Our first session did not go well. Hamid, evidently still affected by his overindulgence the night before, did not perform with the grace and skill he'd once exhibited.

We were gathered in the smaller guest room, where the acoustics are best, Hamid plucking his elegant *temur* and singing his songs of mountain courage, and beside him the two other musicians, one cradling a leather frame-drum and the other coaxing a lament out of an apricot-wood pipe. I stood before them, steadying the recording horn; Aminat stayed back near the door, watching. I had suggested that they rehearse before we imprint a wax disc – they are far too precious to waste – and the troupe complied, but the rehearsal was not promising. This was clearly because of Hamid, and his failure brought shame upon them all. I heard the other two complaining to each other in their local tongue – of which I understood little but the frequent mention of the word 'vodka'. They had guessed at the cause of his weakness. Quite likely they could smell it on him, just as my mother always did when my father took a dram on his way home. I suspect that was why she always demanded a kiss when he came through the door. I used to think it was a sign of her great affection, and maybe it was – they seemed happy enough – but there was a measure of monitoring in it too, I think.

We recorded the performance anyway, despite the poor rehearsal. And it was better this time, perhaps because Hamid was chastened, perhaps because he had sobered up a little. I stood there watching them, but not really watching, for my eyes while open were yet resting, so that my other senses could learn more...not only from the music and Hamid's voice. I became aware of the warmth in the room, the creep of it across the soft floor, towards the cold steel of the weaponry hanging on the wall behind me. I perceived the smell of the men, their sweat, the sweetness of the wood instruments and the leather of the boots collected at the entrance, the richness of the air wafting in from outside, which captured all the earthy smells of the *aul*, of food and dirt and dung. And the scent of the woman behind me, mistress of her own body, the shifting weight of her — I discerned it all, and I wonder if any of this will find its way into my recording, so that its listeners can sense it too, while not knowing what it is that moves them so deeply, imagining it is solely the music, and not understanding that the whole environment in which it was recorded was also in tune.

Afterwards Hamid apologised to me. He was not at his best today, he said. But he was also very sure that his condition would be much worse had I not 'gifted him' (this was the very phrase he used) the night before. The drink, he suggested, had done a great deal to ease his pain, and pain, he declared, is the worst crime that can be inflicted upon music. 'If you wound a musician you wound his people,' he lamented.

'And perhaps the world,' I added, alluding to the global prospects of gramophone technology, and trying to flatter him at the same time.

Hamid nodded — I am not quite sure he understood my meaning. I think he was rather approving of the philosophical sense of my words, that music is a kind of gift, a spiritual essence that enriches humanity. He must be about seventy, and I don't think he can imagine the world beyond his own land, this mound of rock where he has lived his entire life. He is embedded completely in the mountains. But then I can see how easily that might happen.

4

Last time, Hamid told me the story of how he was injured – he was ambushed by Cossacks and gravely wounded fending them off. It was a tale of heroism and bravery, made all the more impressive for the modesty and stoicism he exhibited in its telling. But today a new story has emerged, and a far less noble one at that.

It came to me quite by accident. I had spent the morning in the *aul*, and on a whim decided to go out and buy myself a *burka*. I'd long been admiring these cloaks for their beauty and practicality – the way men twirl the fabric beneath them to create a seat for themselves on the dusty ground. I approached the old man who sits perpetually at the end of the street, like a place marker, to ask how and where I might find one, and he immediately engaged me in a conversation about the household in which I am staying. My host, he confirmed, was injured during the time of the Caucasian Wars. But not in any kind of conflict – in fact, there wasn't a Russian in sight! Rather, it had happened when his horse, spooked by something or other, reared...Hamid's foot was caught in the stirrup, and the distressed creature then ran for several miles, dragging him by his one leg. That is why he limps, that is why he alludes constantly to his pain. It was evident from the old man's tone that Hamid did not command his respect, and that his ordeal was not considered a worthy one.

I did not have to press him to continue – he was like a shrub after the rain that responds to the slightest touch by releasing the shower of drops collected in it. 'And do you know who his wife is?' he asked me. 'She is the daughter of Hadji Zurab. Now, there is a proper *dzhigit!*'

There again was that word I hear so often in these parts. At first I thought it referred to a reckless, even dangerous type, a bandit, and perhaps there is a little of that in it, but now I understand it to be the highest compliment for a man, who must above all be a fine rider to earn the title.

The old man continued: 'Hadji Zurab too was injured, but he was injured fighting. Twice they ran him through with a bayonet, beat him viciously too, and yet still he survived, as he does to this day, but you'll never hear a complaint out of him! And he is not so feeble of spirit as to succumb to the enemy's poison, which the scoundrels introduced to destroy us mountain folk.'

By this I assume he meant vodka. 'But the wars are long over,' I said. 'You live in peace with the Russians. You and all the peoples of this great land, under the protection of the Tsar.'

'For now at least,' he replied. 'But we are old, Hamid and I. We won't see it. We will be dead soon.'

I explained that that was why I had come – to collect his music before it was lost to time. The old man conceded that Hamid was certainly a great musician. 'And when you have collected it,' he asked, 'what further use will he be to you, or you to him?'

He was right, of course. Once I have finished my recording I will leave, and then Hamid will have nobody to assist him with his vice. I can see now that he will string out our sessions for as long as he can, promising much but feeding me only morsels in order to keep me here.

5

I ought to have left by now. I ought not to be here. The company does not know I have returned to Dagestan. According to my schedule I am in Baku now, departing tomorrow for Isfahan. I no longer know how, or if, I will catch up.

6

Last night I drank with Hamid again. He was annoyed at having to share, but pleased with the company. For my part, I reasoned that drinking half the bottle myself would render him less incapacitated the next day. I plan to get one more session out of him today at least, before I take my leave.

But here I must write more of Aminat, who is the centre of the household. She leaves us men be, as a wife should, yet when she goes the room seems depleted somehow. I do not much enjoy sitting here with this old man, listening to his stories, none of which I can now believe are not lies. I sense that Aminat benefits from my presence also. For I have noticed that when Hamid leaves the room — as he does frequently to relieve himself — she appears immediately to check I have everything I need, that the guest is satisfied. Last night she came in wearing the long shirt they call a *beshmet* and an embroidered velvet vest, across which lay a necklace of silver charms and coins. As she knelt beside me to pour more tea I noticed that the coins — of which there were at least ten — were stamped with the Russian eagle. She moved a little closer to me so that I could see better. 'Is it not too heavy?' I inquired, unsure of whether she could understand, for she had never before uttered a word to me.

Her reply surprised me – her Russian is far more advanced than mine. Moreover, she spoke with an astonishing poise. She said: 'It is, sir, yet it is nothing when weighed against my other burdens, which are far heavier.'

Just then my host returned, limping in from the chill night, rubbing his old hands together. I was suddenly overwhelmed with pity for them both, and it was all I could do not to weep.

7

I am still here, of course...

8

Our conversation must have emboldened her, because Aminat has since made several attempts to converse with me, but only in the absence of her husband. In turn I was encouraged to learn that she is the daughter of a great man...that she is educated and different from her husband in many ways. I guess that she is in her mid-thirties, and Hamid has alluded to her having at least one child, a daughter, though the girl does not live here with them. I am not yet so bold as to ask why.

Today, while Hamid was sleeping, Aminat asked me to show her where I have been. I laid my map out on the floor and we knelt over it together, and she watched my finger trace over the paper mountains of the near east, from Svanetia to Batumi to Erivan, and then in a loop around Lake Sevan, which I told her was the prettiest lake in all the world.

Learning this she expressed a desire to see it. 'And where will you go next, after leaving us?' she asked.

'South,' I told her, 'but on further east, to Persia…'

Then, to my surprise, she remarked: 'They say the quality of opium in Persia is the very best.'

I assumed this knowledge to be another marker of her education. 'Perhaps so,' I replied. 'The climate must be good for it there. But Persia is vast, and I suppose some regions cultivate the poppy better than others.'

Aminat then sat back on the balls of her feet. 'It's a pity you are not returning. You might have brought him some.' I did not interject, but allowed her to continue. 'In the past, before our courtship, my husband was an opium user. It suited him well. It dulled his pain and made him more gentle, sweeter. His music was sweeter too. After we married, my father put a stop to it. It is not permitted, you see. My father does not believe a man should be sweet. He says that a man must bear his pain, or he is not a man at all. Yet poor Hamid cannot bear his pain – so it spills over onto me.'

'One can find the drug in these parts also,' I said. 'I have seen great fields of poppies growing outside Derbent.'

'Yes – once my husband had an acquaintance who brought it to him from there. But that man stopped coming…it was not in his interest.' Here she paused. 'Mr Aitken, before you leave us forever, I would ask you a favour – if you would help us as that man once did. Please, find some opium for Hamid, relieve his torment. We would both be indebted to you for this mercy.'

I promised her I would think about it, and give her my answer tomorrow.

9

I am becoming accustomed to this life. This perpetual journeying, the administration of belongings and a tradition that are not my own, being a stranger among strangers, the extremes of hospitality and hostility – neither of which I deserve. Even my body has adapted. After so many hours on horseback I do not ache as I once did, and I am more used to resting my body on hard earth than a soft bed. I am becoming weather-beaten like all the men here, and like them I finally look older than I am, rather than younger, as has been my life's bane up till now. My sense of time has shifted...I am less circumspect, and no longer feel rushed in my journeying. And yet I do not live here, nor anywhere. I am afraid that the concept of home has also become foreign to me. Now, it is only a place to which I might be permitted to return.

10

Before I left for the mission Aminat had asked of me I made the unexpected acquaintance of her father, Hadji Zurab. He came to the house very early in the morning, just as I was loading my horse – had he arrived ten minutes later I would have been gone. He told me he had heard I was leaving and wanted to meet the Englishman before he departed. Here, though I was not a little awed by the great man, I was obliged to correct him. I was Scottish, not

English. This distinction confused him, so I explained it thus: that we on the British Isles also have many clans and tribes. I also assured him that I would be returning soon, but I needed a reason for my brief absence, so I seized on the fiction that I was merely going on a short music-gathering expedition. Of course, I could not then leave without my equipment, so went to fetch it and load it onto my horse, all the while under Hadji Zurab's interested gaze. He was satisfied with my story, and insisted that I come and see him as soon as I returned, and to bring along the music I had collected with me. I explained that I did not have the means to play back what I had recorded, and so the music would remain trapped in the discs until they arrived back in Tiflis. 'Never mind,' he said. 'Come anyway. You will be the first emissary of your clan.' I accepted and mounted my horse. Aminat and her father bade me a successful journey and stood watching as I rode away from the *aul*. Hamid, of course, slept through the whole thing.

II

The magnificence of Derbent must be qualified by the fact that I was nearly killed there. I was approaching the gates of the ancient citadel, wondering about all the barbarians it has kept out – and those it has failed to – when a pair of scoundrels descended upon me. With their dirty, matted *papakhi* on their heads they appeared as wild dogs, and they clawed at the flank of my horse, trying to pull me off. They succeeded. As I fell to the ground I heard something inside of me crack, and a pain shot through my shoulder, to which the brutes added many more, the one assailing me with blows while the other steadied my horse. I could hear the excitement in their voices...most likely they were celebrating the capture of a foreigner, and the strange and heavy load he carried. They would have abducted me for sure – my principal assailant was already trying to lift my broken body onto his horse – when a group of locals approached, running to my aid. My attackers abandoned me at once, leaving me crumpled on the path. But I was safe, as was the money I'd wisely strapped around my waist before leaving. My horse and equipment, however, were gone.

I was taken into a private home, undressed, and my wounds attended to. The money was removed from my person, but placed on the floor beside me. My pockets had been emptied and these belongings too were laid out neatly where I could see them. Among them had been the instructions Aminat had given me. Soon a young man, evidently the only one in the family who spoke Russian, came to me with the note in his hands. 'You want opium?' he asked. Too concussed to explain myself, and too paralysed by pain, I only nodded. A few hours later I was awoken by the sound of a lamp and pipe being set up nearby. I had seen men use these before, and did not need any instruction. I turned on my side, took the pipe, in which the tacky cone bubbled away like a tiny volcano, and inhaled deeply.

It was extraordinary...the relief was immediate. Suddenly I could see my good fortune for what it was...I felt as if I were an infant again, being cared for in the bosom of my own family. I exhaled, a blue vapour poured from me, and in it I felt a sense that I was divesting myself only of the most onerous aspects of my existence – of pain, of sensation, of emotion. I thought then of Hamid, and felt for the first time that he was not my subject, nor my rival, but my brother.

12

I am told that Aminat's father was about to send an envoy out to search for me, I was gone so long. Nearly a week I spent in the home of my rescuers, in that beautiful blue haze, before I was sufficiently recovered to make my way back to the *aul*. Without any effort on my part I had found the opium dealer Aminat had asked me to and procured the desired quantity. Anticipating my own use in the days ahead, however, I doubled my purchase. Other costs went to my hosts, partly in gratitude, partly for the opium I had already consumed, and also for the hire of a new horse and rider who would ensure my safe passage home. My expense fund from the company is now greatly reduced. My equipment is gone. Yet I no longer feel adrift.

13

Hadji Zurab says I am not to leave until I am fully recovered. He is appalled by what happened to me; he interrogated me for some time about my assailants, and speaks of having them found and dealt with in the harshest terms. I do not believe he is as powerful as that, and I have no interest in helping him in this. I do not want him meddling…I do not want to be indebted to him. He does not know the real purpose of my journey to Derbent, and were he to find out, we would all three of us suffer, Hamid, Aminat and I.

14

I am more well-disposed towards Hamid now. And he has softened – the opium takes the rough edges off him, and perhaps me also, so that when we sit smoking together, taking turns with the pipe, there is no friction, no greed, no impatience. The drug quietens him, too – when he is smoking he is wordlessly content...it obliterates his pain, that thing that has defined him for so long. I understand him better when he does not speak to me.

It is not all silence. At times he picks up his instrument, and sometimes he sings also. With my equipment gone I know he is playing only for the pleasure of it – for that which it gives us all. Aminat is right, his music is sweeter now. And though I cannot record it for the world to hear, it no longer seems to matter very much. When we smoke, Aminat leaves us be, and ensures that visitors are not admitted. But when Hamid plays she returns...she sits with me and we watch her husband, with his eyes closed and his old man's fingers dancing over the *temur*'s strings. He is enveloped in a strange calm. I glance at Aminat, and she too has changed. She is brimming with joy, and her joy spills over onto me.

The sting

Narva, Estonia, 1919

I thought she might resist me, but she does not. She unbuttons her shirt as I instruct, revealing her small, mole-speckled breasts, then shifts her bottom for me to pull off her underpants. She shivers a little as I descend upon her, and as I prise open her legs and her sex, and I push myself inside. She is holding her breath, as if this will still time, as if this will preserve her chastity. It will not. I am not gentle – I don't believe it helps a girl to be eased into slowly – it only prolongs the discomfort. I fuck her to my pleasure, as I will from now on, and as other men will after me. This is better for us both.

She does not cry, as girls often do. But this is wartime, and she is a fighter, and she wants me to think that she is strong. I come quickly – more quickly than I would like, but it cannot be helped – and as I pull out of her I spill my seed on the floor between her legs and some on her bandages, too. I am not usually so messy.

'I'll change them,' I gasp, catching my breath. 'It's not hygienic.' I will have to clean the floor as well before my next patient comes in.

They brought her to me a week ago. She had been shot in the leg and was wearing the standard uniform of the Finnish Volunteer Corps. Her hair was cut short and she was tiny under that great coat, in those snow-rotted boots. But she had done a good job – I did not spot right away that she was a girl and neither, it seemed, had any of the men with whom she'd been fighting. She just looked like one of those pretty young fellows of whom there are so many, who join up hoping that war will propel them more swiftly into manhood. Some it does, some it doesn't. I'm not quite sure how it works for a young woman.

On that first meeting, while I was still under the fiction of her masculinity, she told me her name was Eljas, that she was nineteen and had served in the liberation of her own nation before coming to help us with ours. I unwrapped the dressing that someone on the field had hastily – and badly – applied, and examined the wound. She was lucky: the bullet had entered just above the kneecap and lodged in muscle instead of bone. I cleaned the wound and removed the bullet, sterilised it and packed the hole with gauze. Her eyes were closed; when I finished she let out a big sigh.

'Since you are so experienced in military matters,' I asked her then, 'which war do you prefer – yours or ours?'

'Neither,' she answered. 'I prefer peace.' That seemed a sensible answer, but then she added: 'In peacetime there is always the anticipation of the next war.' It was at that point I suspected something wasn't quite right.

This was confirmed when, her leg newly bandaged, I ordered her to submit to an overall examination. She hesitated before undressing, but when she did, it only revealed more bandages, these ones strapped across her chest. 'Another injury?' I asked, and she nodded, but I could see that wasn't it. It was then that the first glimmer of truth appeared to me. I'd had an intuition of her sex before I knew it rationally, like an animal that catches the scent of wounded prey, and only has to go a few more steps to find it lying there, trembling, waiting to be devoured. It was terribly exciting, this frisson of possibility.

I stepped forward. 'Let's have a look,' I said, and she edged away from me warily. 'Stay still, Private. That is an order!' I snapped. 'Now raise your arms!' She did as she was told. I unsecured the binding at her chest, then walked around her, circling her slowly, unravelling her lie. Oh, how I enjoyed that. And at the end the fabric fell away and her hands flew to her chest, over the buds of her womanhood. 'Well, well, well,' I said.

That was when she confessed. Her real name is Elli, she is from Karelia, the third daughter of a farming family. She did serve in the Finnish civil war, but as a nurse. Yet she wanted so desperately to fight, she became a man and joined the volunteers instead.

'And what do you think about being a man?' I asked her. 'Does it agree with you?'

'I like to be useful,' she replied.

'Are nurses not useful?'

'Our armies need fighters more than those who just pick up the pieces.'

I saw then that she was not one to give an intelligent answer. 'Well,' I said, 'you won't be very useful to any army now. Not until this heals. But you might be extremely useful to me.'

'I told you I don't want to be a nurse.'

'That wasn't what I had in mind,' I said.

That was when we came to our arrangement. I would treat her and keep her secret for her, so she could return to the field later on, if only she would do some small favours for me. I wonder now, as I bend over her, changing the semen-stained dressing for a new one, if she has any idea what she has got herself into.

Tonight I am troubled, I cannot sleep. I foolishly sent her back to the ward with the men, and now I fear she will be found out. She has been among them for weeks, and none have detected her lie, but now her situation has changed. She is injured and vulnerable. She has the aura of sex about her. And she is a woman in a way she wasn't before, which is of course entirely down to me. I resolve that tomorrow I will get her out of there. I will diagnose her as having an infectious condition, and I will put her in isolation. That is the only way, I think.

In the morning I go to her. She is sitting up in bed, with breakfast on her lap, and still has sleep about her. It is a particularly feminine drowsiness, and I can see now, as I could not before – even as I was deflowering her, for the remnants of maleness still adhered to her then – that she has a unique quality. I have had many women, and quite a few of them patients, so I do not think it is merely the weakness of convalescence that appeals. My judgement is quite objective. But I do admit that it may be something to do with the revelation of her sex in the midst of all these male bodies – one is struck more by one's good fortune when one does not expect it. I smile at her as I approach, and she wipes a smear of strawberry jam from her lips with the back of her hand, an uncouth and boyish gesture for the benefit of the others, not for me. She offers a tentative smile back. *Oh*, I think, *but this one is all mine.*

I moved her in good time, as there are a lot of nurses doing their rounds. The men are one thing, but Elli has already shown that she can deceive them. Women are quite another; since they are themselves always prowling for males, they are able to detect an imposter in their midst.

She is all alone in the annex where we put infectious cases. Of course, with a treasure kept in a box one has to open it from time to time just to reassure oneself that it is still there. Over the next few days I visit her often, whenever I can. I do not waste such opportunities, and she knows each time I come in what I have come for, and she keeps her part of the bargain. When I fuck her she behaves as if it were merely a part of her treatment: I undress her, arrange her in positions convenient to my access (trying not to aggravate the injury), issue the occasional instruction and then quickly and efficiently carry out my duties.

Somehow she understands all this to be necessary. Soldiers, I have always said, make the best patients – they are used to following orders, to relinquishing control of their bodies. Each time I come in I give her a new command, and she fulfils it without complaint. After three days, there is not an inch of her I do not know, and I reach the satisfying but melancholy goal of having completely exhausted my imagination. And then she says to me, 'I had no idea a doctor's training was so thorough.' The cheeky little bitch.

She would have me be more thorough still. Today I am weary from a long day of consultations, crises and decisions, and content to revert to the missionary position. I collapse onto her and rock thoughtlessly, blissfully inside her until, at the point where I am approaching climax, she suddenly reaches up, grabs my hand and guides it to her wound. The dressing has already been loosened, and as I am on the edge she presses my fingers into the sticky opening. I pull out of her only just in time.

She does not, or cannot, say why she did it. Still dazed, I inspect the wound, which has begun bleeding again. 'It was healing so nicely too,' I say ruefully. But I'm not sure I want her to heal too quickly, so the next time she does it, I let her. Once again she thrusts my fingers into the fissure in her leg, and holds them there as I shudder my finish. Somehow it pleases her, and somehow this pleases me. After the third time, the wound becomes infected. I have done my best to penetrate her cleanly (I wash my hands before our encounters, as I do with all my other patients) but I cannot say it surprises me. What we have done goes against all good practice. Yet her taking my hand and bringing it to her moves me. It is her sole act, the sole intimation that she wants me there. I must cure her — the infection might be fatal — but I will feel the loss of this strange affection. Lying in the afterglow of our union I tell her that I will not, I cannot, do this again.

The wound, once so clean and uncomplicated, has become difficult to treat. I try applying different solutions, but progress is slow. Elli and I discuss her condition together – after all, she knows a little about nursing – and she tells me that there is one thing we haven't tried yet: the venom of a bee, which, she says, can cure many ills.

'What a ridiculous notion,' I scoff, 'but one that I suppose I should not be surprised to hear, coming from a girl who thinks it is amusing to introduce foreign bodies into her own damaged tissue.'

Elli, however, remains quite insistent about the efficacy of the so-called treatment. 'At home,' she says, 'we wouldn't hesitate. We'd take a couple of bees and make them sting around the infection. It works three ways. Firstly, the venom contains all kinds of healing substances. Secondly, the sting promotes inflammation in the nearby tissue, which helps the body to heal itself. And thirdly, the heat it puts into the skin is also very healing.'

She is evidently proud of her quasi-scientific explanation, and so I do not dismiss her immediately, though the idea is as preposterous as any I have heard. The next day, although I detect no improvement, I patiently listen as she begs me again to just try, to just bring her a few harmless bees. 'I'm telling you it won't work,' I say, and for the first time I see tears in her eyes. She is frightened, she says; she does not want to die. Though it is entirely her fault she is in this fix, I take pity on her. I do not want her to die either. I agree to bring her some bees, but only if she is sensible about administering the venom. She agrees, and I am relieved too that the matter is resolved. I lie down on the thin strip of bed next to her and push my fingers into her cunt, and she lets out that deep, exhausted sort of sigh.

When I bring them to her – four black bees in a jar – she is as delighted as if she had received a real gift. She thanks me, then wiggles herself into position. 'Help me,' she says, and I prop her up and pull back the sheets. She unscrews the jar, taps one of the bees out onto a piece of card and carefully transfers it to her leg. The bee, evidently disoriented, crouches still for a moment, then begins the difficult trek across the downy hair of her thigh.

'How do you get it to sting you?' I whisper.

'I insult it,' she whispers back, and then with her fingernail gently flicks the bee on its wing. Immediately it plunges its stinger into her flesh, leaving the tiny barb embedded there, and then stumbles off to die.

'She sacrificed herself for me,' Elli says, satisfied.

'Only because you tricked her,' I reply, picking up the doomed creature and placing it in my palm.

The following day Elli provokes two more stings on her leg – one in the morning and one in the evening. The limb is now extremely warm, tight and swollen, but I cannot tell that it has done the wound any good. It looks ugly, quite deformed. 'Enough,' I tell her. 'I'll have no further part in it.' I ignore her pleading, take the jar with the last remaining bee and return to my room.

This is the first day I have not touched her, except to tend to her injury, and now that I am lying alone in my bed

I regret it deeply. One day soon Elli will be gone – she will either be dead or cured, but either way, she will be gone. Today her body was so assaulted, so compromised, and her thoughts so distant from mine, that I could not find the space nor the sense for fucking. But now, here in my room, there is nothing but space. I am consumed by the need to fill her with me, to brace her body to mine, and in return she would consume part of this emptiness that surrounds me.

The next morning when I unlock the door to the isolation ward there is a young man in there. Not a young woman pretending to be a young man, but a real soldier, who stirs as I enter. He coughs. 'I'd keep my distance if I were you, Doc,' and I take a step back out of the miasmic air and close the door again. Then I walk up and down the empty corridor for a while. I walk and walk and do not stop until a hand touches my shoulder. 'Everything all right, Doctor?' a voice says, and I realise I have been pacing almost blindly with my head in my hands. It is one of the nurses. 'Are you feeling all right, Dr Kask?' she asks with professional concern. It is from her that I learn that Elli was moved in the night, and that Dr Härma authorised it. That I should see Dr Härma if I'm at all concerned.

I catch Härma coming out of the bathroom. 'Mikhel!' he greets me, patting his hands dry on his coat. 'To what do I owe the pleasure?'

He knows very well. 'I was just wondering,' I said, 'about the patient in isolation.'

'Private Lippmaa? He was brought in late last night. Suspected cholera.'

'I rather meant the one who was in there before.'

'Oh, you mean the Finnish girl? She is not infectious. I moved her.'

'Where to, where is she now?'

'Well, now, my friend, I'm wondering if that is something you really ought to know.'

'She is' – oh, how I do swallow my pride – 'still my patient, and she is still undergoing treatment.'

'Perhaps,' Härma says, 'you would tell me what kind of treatment involves bee stings? Your girl was admitted two weeks ago with a simple flesh wound – it should be much improved by now, and it is plainly not. While you are at it, you might also explain to me why you isolated a non-infectious patient and, on discovering her sex, did not transfer her to the women's ward.'

Feebly I told him that the bees had been her idea, that I too had thought it a strange custom, but that she'd insisted on them so strongly that I consented. The other matters did not really need explaining. Härma knows exactly why I isolated her. I do have something of a reputation.

'She has been moved on for her safety,' he says. 'You are not to know where. The nurses will not tell you. And if you try to find out you can be sure that an account of your sordid arrangement will find its way to the Director.' I must look rather pathetic, because he adds, 'I will tell you this – she is to be sent back to Finland as soon as she is recovered.'

'So she will recover?' I ask.

'For your sake,' he replies, 'I hope so.'

It is a very long day, with many patients to see – there was firefight along the river, and now the casualties are coming in. Yet I do not talk to anyone beyond what is necessary, and I avoid looking a single person in the eye. At the end of it I return, exhausted, to my office. The snow has stopped falling; the cold empty night has long settled in. On my desk is the jar with the black bee inside. She is still alive, but sits passively at the base. Such a short life, and so much of it lived in captivity. I put the jar in my bag and take it home.

I lie naked and still in the semi-darkness, throbbing with an indistinct pain. The window is open, and cold air is slowly filling the room. The jar is on my bedside table, and the warmth of the lamplight seems to have roused the bee, which has begun to hum softly inside. I reach over and take the jar and balance it on my bare chest, its wiry hairs flattened beneath the glass. The bee is walking around the base. I watch her a while, then tilt the jar, remove the lid and let her out onto my skin. Whether she will take flight and live her last few hours in freedom or stay in the warmth and die with me, I will soon know.

10

Pilgrimage in light

Cebu City, Philippines, 1970

On the screen is a man's body, pudgy and supple as dough. Over him stands the healer; he lays his hands on the man and begins to knead his torso, shoulders, arms. After a while, he stops and his hands settle just above the man's navel. Here, the healer begins to pinch and prise at the skin, his fingers coming together at the tips, like some fossicking creature, as blood begins to well up between those fingers, now disappearing as if into the abdominal cavity.

Still, his hands work at a startling pace, he seems to be clawing at the man's viscera, and there is yet more blood, which the healer smears over the wobbling, assailed belly at the same time as he pulls out a thread of dark tissue, something clotted and elastic. With one hand he extracts the matter, and with the other keeps working away in the pool of blood. The viewers can't help but be struck by how dextrous he is. Now comes more glutinous tissue, dark purple specks of gunk that the healer also produces before laying them out on the man's chest.

The process has all the urgency and efficiency of a factory production line – a swift sorting out of good from bad, removing the defective tissue, the stuff that undermines the whole. Nevertheless, the psychic surgeon, as he calls himself, cannot quite shake his resemblance to a plumber overcoming a particularly persistent blockage. The patient, his eyes still closed, and his palms upturned at his sides, is unfazed by it all. Though no anaesthetic has been used he lies calmly. He seems not to be feeling a thing.

There. The last slimy clots and strings have been laid out, and the healer's fingers become visible again, as if they've emerged from the fissure they made earlier. He steps away so that his assistant can wipe down the whole bloody, quivering surface, and when the towels have mopped up the muck, the bar's patrons see that the skin over the man's abdomen is as intact as it was before – no wound, no scar, no bleeding. Not a trace of what has just occurred. The healer places his palms an inch over the man, issues a prayer in song – or at least the strained half-talking, half-singing of someone who is tone deaf – and when he is done the man sits up, pats his belly, smiles in an uncertain, confused kind of way, and says thanks.

There is a brief silence in the bar while the patrons weigh up what they have just seen. And in this silence Ambrosio considers the performance too, and what he is thinking is, *That doesn't look so hard.*

Twenty-one or so years earlier, Ambrosio's mother Letty, while pregnant with him, visited a *mananambal*, a folk healer, to ensure that her child would be healthy, intelligent and good-looking. She was not disappointed. Baby Ambrosio was a chubby joy – he slept well, fed well, sailed through infancy with little more than a cough, and the promise of his beautiful, expressive face would be fulfilled in the handsome and confident young man he'd become. She consulted a healer again later, too, when she was carrying his brother, but the results weren't so impressive the second time. Though Fernando was also healthy, he was fairly ordinary as far as the rest was concerned. The spirits must have put all of their power into perfecting her first-born, so that by the time little Fernando came along, there wasn't much left for him.

Letty was by far the most striking woman in the neighbourhood. She was not, perhaps, what they call a natural beauty, but she knew how to work with what she had. When she made herself a dress, she added a flourish – a well-placed split, a lace trim, a rose artfully constructed from scraps of ribbon, a pleating around the bust. On a stand by the doorway she kept a mirror and a pot of lipstick; before opening the door to visitors she anointed her face three times, once on each cheek and then on the lips, crossing herself, almost. She presented herself as a gift to all who laid eyes on her.

Not everyone could recognise her generosity, however. Her misfortunes she attributed to the evil eye; this was the eternal problem of attractive women. But the sin of envy was the burden of the one who had cast it. Pity, and prayers – if they had not wounded her too badly, that was what they would get from her in return.

The most important thing was that she was never ignored, and that was the lesson she taught her sons, too:

not to become lazy, not to settle for merely blending in. Not to be mediocre, and never to be ordinary. There was no excuse for it. Even if the world was against you and resources were few, everyone could do something to distinguish themselves. It was a question of will, resourcefulness and hard work. Of charity, and of love. 'The world can be ugly,' she said, 'but if we accept that ugliness we injure others as well as ourselves. And we injure God, who went to all the trouble of making us, so the least we can do is trouble ourselves to refine His work. For each of us has the responsibility to show the best of ourselves to the world. And in so doing, we come a little bit closer to *realising* that best version − you need to look the part before you can become it.'

Letty's sons owed it to her, too; she hadn't exactly had an easy time bringing them into the world, which she didn't do just so she could add a couple more average Joes clogging up the streets. Because humanity is on the whole mediocre, disappointing and underwhelming, and you do everyone a favour if you raise the average.

Fernando, content with his mediocrity and ill-equipped to overcome it in any case, we will leave here. But don't worry about Fernando − he is living a good, quiet life, he has his own sons now, and his mother still loves him, despite his shortcomings. Ambrosio, however, took her lesson to heart, and ploughed all his efforts into improving the excellent template God had provided. He began from a very young age, training his muscles by lifting things found on the street − water-filled bottles or old tyres. He did not overindulge with food or even, later on, with alcohol. He took care to scrub his face, comb his hair and wear shoes, even when the other boys didn't. This extra bit of effort went down very well with the opposite sex, and by the age of twenty he'd had that same number of girls. Yet he treated them with more decency than they were accustomed to, giving them as much attention as he gave himself, so that they did not feel like one of a number of conquests, but instead, if only briefly, the centre of a beautiful and refined world, and it pleased them to have a reason to care about themselves, to see someone else interested in the project of their making. And so it caught on, as the other boys observed Ambrosio's success, eventually conceding the benefits of personal grooming and good manners and, as a result, the whole tenor of the neighbourhood improved. An entire generation had been saved because of the high standards Ambrosio had set. You can imagine how proud that made his mother.

But a good man's work is never done. Suddenly, young Ambrosio's future was splayed in two: one of his girls fell pregnant at the same time as an opportunity to travel arose. Though the destination was Vietnam, at that time a rapidly escalating war zone, the timing seemed opportune. Ambrosio wouldn't have to fight, only work in the Civic Action Group, a support unit of medical personnel, engineers, trainers and so on that his government had offered when called upon by its American allies. It didn't take him very long to decide to go. He'd done much for his community, had done much for that girl, but staying now would stifle his development – he had more to give than that. God had opened up this path for him, nudged him down it. By the summer of 1968 Ambrosio had joined the group as a cook, and was busy preparing variations on pork, beans and rice for his countrymen at their base near Saigon. For this work he had his mother's blessing.

And that might have been it. Ambrosio might have seen out his tour and returned safe and sound to Cebu, to a life of hard work, easy seduction and modest, charisma-driven good fortune. His mother's advice had always concerned living in the present, and so he hadn't much bothered to consider his future; he'd always left God, who was more capable, to do that. He trusted the Lord would show the way; what he did on that path, however, he knew was up to him.

Yet even if he had considered the future it would not have turned out as he'd imagined. Three months before the Filipino withdrawal, a fight broke out in a crowded bar in Saigon. Ambrosio was there – he had entered with his friends, looking as splendid as he had ever done, and exited with a broken nose, ruptured left eye, and mild concussion. His best shirt ruined. When he awoke the next afternoon, examining the damage in a mirror (it looked and felt as though his head had been dropped from a great height), and saw that his crucifix and St Christopher charms were gone, torn off in the melee, his faith did falter briefly. Why that marine had lunged at him, tried to mess up that pretty face, Ambrosio was not sure. Perhaps it had something to do with a woman, perhaps not.

The punch had split open his eyeball, switching it off completely. The eye, they said, was irreparably damaged – he would never see out of it again. In the weeks that followed, Ambrosio tried to resign himself to this half-vision, a world torn off at the edge. As the tissue gradually healed, and the pain subsided, his loss became more real. It was as if a precipice had opened up beside him, one-dimensional, yet with a darkness that was alive and weighty, as though it was a kind of cosmic mass interfering with the matter surrounding it, upsetting all balance and equilibrium. He forced himself to kneel as he prayed, despite the spinning and the feeling that he would tip over. He thanked God for preserving his other eye, that he might still see the beauty in the world, as well as its terror.

But God was even more gracious than that. On the eve of the withdrawal, Ambrosio's ruptured eye began to flicker back into life. It began as a hazy light, like that of daybreak, when the air is moist and subtly sweet. He wondered if it was the stress of preparing to leave, but several days later, after he'd arrived back in Cebu, he found he could also determine colours, as well as the faint outlines of things. Soon, the shapes became clearer, even identifiable. He was defying the medics, who with their pessimistic predictions had got it completely wrong. Yet neither did he see as he had before. Everything that registered through the injured eye had a luminous, otherworldly sheen, as if his retina were mother-of-pearl, lifted out of the depths and now reflecting everything in a mysterious light. These impressions overlapped with the sight in his good eye, so that now everything he saw, though fragmented, took on an unreal quality, a radiance that it had not had before.

And then came the visions. From the damaged eye emerged images of things that were not there, and these too were projected onto this new world. He saw tiny people sprouting from the ground like mushrooms; water flowing down a street, transforming it into a river (a vision so real it even had detritus bobbing in it); he saw his father, who had died a long time ago, and who now looked gentle, almost timid; he saw the Archangel St Michael, porcelain white, though he was kneeling in the mud.

Late one night, Ambrosio found a litter of puppies at the end of his bed. In a panic he tried to kick them off; the puppies became blurry for a moment but would not budge, and the delusion stubbornly remained until he threw aside the sheet and leaned forward to uproot the phantasmic creatures, to scatter the snug, gently writhing mass. Then the next morning he woke to find miniature storm clouds gathering beneath the ceiling, and he wondered if this was an admonition for dislodging the puppies. He knew that neither the clouds nor the dogs were real, but he did not know why they had appeared, and it frightened him.

Only after some time did he come to understand that they were simply visual hallucinations, harmless figments. And when he did, he was able to welcome his visitations. Though they were random, sometimes banal, there was a numinous quality to them. Animals and insects, people and saints, mountains and moons, elaborate scenes and simple patterns all wavered into his consciousness, investing those moments with something unknowable and sacred. Perhaps this was what his mother had meant about overcoming mediocrity. Perhaps God was showing him how mundane bodily misfortune might be transformed into something unique and revelatory.

Ambrosio did not tell anyone about the hallucinations, or his chosenness, until long after he returned from Vietnam. Knowing what dark forces envy could inspire in men, he learnt to interpret his visions in private, not ignoring but not acknowledging them either when others were around. There was a great satisfaction to be had in seeing what nobody else could.

Of course, he could not keep the secret from his mother. She had seen him trying to shoo away a small pig that was standing on its hind legs, begging for scraps. 'Sorry, Mama, I can't get rid of it,' he said when she came in, catching him waving his arms at thin air; this vision, so incredibly vivid, had sneaked in under his radar. But it was a relief to tell her, and she listened calmly as he described all the things he'd seen that were not really there. Letty stroked his brow over his ruined eye, her lovely boy no longer so lovely, and thought for a few minutes about what he had told her. 'It sounds harmless,' she concluded, 'but go ask the *mananambal* just in case.'

The local healer lived in the block of flats across the road, his window almost facing theirs. As that window was rarely opened, his rooms had become an archive of smells amassed over the years – tobacco, cooked meat and boiled plant matter. The healer was a plump man, apparently not fond of the purging remedies he was known to prescribe. Ambrosio sat opposite him, gazing over his shoulder at the lacy curtains of his mother's window. He saw her figure standing there, but for a moment wasn't entirely sure if it was her or an illusion, the glass at the healer's was so grimy, and before he had a chance to figure it out she was gone.

The healer quickly assessed his condition. 'This is a simple case of a hex,' he said. 'Someone doesn't like you and has placed a curse on you. Most likely a love rival, or the family of a girl you've put in the family way and not married.'

This, Ambrosio knew, was a pointed judgement. The girl he'd got pregnant just before leaving for Vietnam also lived in the neighbourhood, and he and his mother, being a cut above the ordinary, were well known in the area. Healers could be such moralistic types. 'And what about your mother, have you been respecting her?' he pressed. 'And your father, visiting his grave? It wouldn't help if you got on the wrong side of the spirits too,' he added.

'My sins aside,' Ambrosio said, 'what can you do for me?' Saying this he noticed that upon the healer's shoulders two dung beetles had appeared, one on either side of his head, and they were lumbering to and fro, each with their small ball of shit. They were slightly out of sync, clumsy and cute. Ambrosio watched with a wry smile, but this the healer took as a smirk, which annoyed him even more, and he recommended a long, apparently punitive course of purging and praying, as well as the purchase of an amulet carved from a blessed stone that Ambrosio was informed he must never remove, but also never get wet. All for a grand total of twenty *pesos*.

'For that,' Ambrosio said, 'for that I could see a doctor twice over, *and* he'd throw in some real medication.'

'You could go to a doctor a hundred times over, but he would not lift your curse,' the healer snapped back. 'And sure, medicine might help with the symptoms, but you'll still be stuck with the hex. Look,' he said, 'I can do you for eighteen.'

Ambrosio told him he would go away and think about it, but they both knew he would not return. Ambrosio did not believe, and if you didn't believe, it wouldn't work. He did not believe because the force of his visions was more compelling than anything the healer could say to him; they had already proved themselves stronger than the promises of the medics who told him he'd never see from that eye again. The visions spoke to him, they were prophetic. And though they might trouble him from time to time, he could not really believe they were any kind of curse.

Now they were coming more often. After the dung beetles, Ambrosio saw an eagle at his own feet – a small one, only about the size of a pigeon (things often came in miniature), and feeding like a pigeon too, pecking at some invisible grain. Eagles – strong birds, symbols of power and perspicacity. The seed – abundance, of course. The eagle was by his side; it held the promise of something. Ambrosio began to suspect that his visions were not as random as they'd at first seemed, but rather symbols or messages that revealed some higher truth.

That afternoon he went for a long walk around the neighbourhood, taking care to avoid both his mother, who would expect a comprehensive report, and Elvira, the mother of his child. He didn't feel good about avoiding Elvira and the little boy, whom he hadn't even met yet, but he knew he wasn't ready. He now had the strong sense that he had to fulfil his own potential before he could help another human with theirs. And that his potential was far greater than he'd imagined, than even his mother had told him.

Apart from the strange embellishments his delusions added, the old *barrio* was much as it had been when he'd left for Vietnam. By the time he arrived home that evening dusk was falling, and always, in the gloom, the visions grew stronger. At his mother's door he found ships rocking on the concrete step, speckled with lights, as if inhabited by tiny sailors. Ambrosio stepped over them and went inside.

'Twenty *pesos!*' his mother exclaimed. 'You were right to walk away. That fatso is a crook. What does he know anyway?'

'Mother,' sighed Ambrosio, 'it was you who sent me there.'

She waved her hand dismissively. 'Well, I was wrong. You know, he's the one I saw when I was carrying your brother too...' She trailed off, not wanting to say it, but the implication was clear – *and you can see how that turned out*. 'I'm sorry, my boy, it was a waste of time. A hex, how ridiculous! Did you tell him about St Michael, or the flowers in the ocean, the light you see in the mirror? It's obviously a gift from Our Father. You have only to figure out what to do with it, how you will fulfil the promise of His Love.'

Ambrosio's new career did not take long to establish. In Manila there were plenty of street psychics, but not so many in Cebu, where he could easily carve out a niche for himself. He wasn't a wizened old woman, like the clairvoyants who read palms in the plazas, or an illiterate village *mananambal*, or a puffed-up city quack like the one across the road. Neither was he a well-trained priest, confident in the dispensation of ready-made platitudes. He was something entirely new, which Cebuanos had never seen before: a young, strong, commanding presence, a man who was marked by fate but who also had been blessed with good looks and extraordinary gifts, who saw spirits and signs everywhere he went, and who knew how to interpret them. At once a healer, a psychic and a man of God, Ambrosio was utterly unique.

His first client came with little effort on his part. He had been walking around the city, looking for a spot to set up his business – all he needed was a space for two stools (he aspired to a small table too, when business picked up) – but it was rainy season and that day's hopes of finding anywhere had been washed away. Soaked to the skin, he sought shelter in a café with a bright-yellow chicken at the entrance – not a vision, but rather a painting on a plank of driftwood nailed over the door. The owner, a stocky middle-aged woman, stepped back when he approached; she had been watching the rain fall, and hadn't even noticed him emerge from it. There was no one else in the café, but she led him to a seat anyway, asking absently what she could get him, for she seemed keener to return to the doorway and gaze into the downpour than attend to any customer. Ambrosio slicked back his hair, the water running in rivulets down the back of his neck, and as he looked at her he noticed her own hair, so thin he could see through it to her freckled scalp, yet defiantly piled high into a fragile beehive. It had a silvery sheen, and there seemed to be small figures moving around in it. Catching him staring at her, the woman became unnerved.

'Wha-what is it?' she asked.

'You have angels in your hair,' Ambrosio whispered.

'What?'

'Yes.' He nodded, although he hadn't really determined what the figures were – they might just as well have been ants – and staring into her hair was actually blurring things rather than making them clearer; the vision was already starting to fade. 'Tiny angels, dancing. You should be glad, it's a sign of very good fortune.'

'How do you figure that?' she said, lifting one hand to fix her hair, and then, suddenly worried that she might disturb the angels, pulling it away again.

'I see it,' he explained, touching the new, larger crucifix on his breastbone. 'God took my eye and in its place put a second sight. With *this* eye' – he pointed to his good one – 'I see the ordinary world, like you do. With *this* one' – he pointed to the other – 'I see the spirits, the saints and the future and' – he paused, aware that this was the moment he was declaring his new vocation – 'with this knowledge I advise and heal.' The owner was about to ask her next question when Ambrosio said, 'You know, I'd love a soda.'

She nodded and went to get one, then hurried back, sitting down opposite him to hear more about her prosperity, which couldn't come soon enough. Ambrosio took a long sip of his drink and then reached out to place her hand between his palms. Gently he stroked down across her knuckles to her fingertips and began to tell her what he saw. A change in her fortunes. A serendipitous visit. An important decision, in which she must err on the side of instinct.

That was the start of it. Having convinced her of his powers, Ambrosio struck a deal with Roza Flores that if she would let him operate out of her café, then he would keep a lookout for her angels, and update her regularly on her progress towards good fortune. Overcoming her husband's objections, which were based mainly on having such a handsome and charming young man installed on the premises, Roza agreed. Naturally, then, with such a handsome and charming young man installed on the premises, business improved greatly, and Ambrosio's first prophecy was fulfilled.

It was gratifying work at first – much safer than cooking in a war zone, more varied, and the customers happier with the service. Sometimes they didn't want to leave at all but just sit there with the young mystic, having him caress their hands and gaze attentively at and around them with an intimacy that was pleasantly unnerving, until a vision that he could read finally emerged. When it did, Ambrosio would tell his client a story that wove the bare strands of what they'd already told him with the hallucination he experienced in their presence. In this way it was not so unlike his previous job – creating something palatable out of just a few ingredients.

An old woman who was accompanied by a snake crawling on the table he advised to beware of people who were out to deceive her (had she been younger, the snakes could have warned of an unscrupulous lover instead). To a policeman with soft green waves lapping silently behind him, Ambrosio suggested he had better prepare for a sea journey (since he couldn't swim, the policeman went away in mild terror). An awkward young seminarian was content to hear that the headaches he'd been having were most likely related to the rainclouds that appeared behind him, and which were probably an indicator of the great and important responsibility he was about to inherit.

The prophecies were very brief and rather vague, but people would gladly pay a few *pesos* to hear about the visions that surrounded them and revealed the truth of their lives, which then seemed richer and so more hopeful. Occasionally Ambrosio would sell an amulet or charm, but only if a customer insisted on one, for he knew in his heart that they did not work, simply because they did not have the authority of a vision. Sometimes, too, a customer would offer him extra money to visit them in their home and lay his hands directly on their affliction, and sometimes he would go, particularly if the person asking was a woman, which was more often than not the case. He didn't know if this treatment was effective either, but from time to time he would oblige.

There was the occasional occupational hazard. He might be visited by a disgruntled husband, or by customers who insisted on wringing more prophecy out of him than he had to give. They could become quite aggressive, these people, needling him for ever more specific details about when they could expect their bright futures to manifest. Ambrosio had to explain, again and again, that fate was like the weather – there were clues to help in forecasting, but the end result was in God's hands, just as no one could predict the precise formations of the clouds, their height and movement and density. Sometimes a vision simply refused to appear, and he couldn't do a reading at all, so he'd have to send the customer away feeling even more abandoned than before. But the poor, sick and lovelorn can be extraordinarily pushy, and they began to grind him down. After almost a year in Roza's café, Ambrosio started to wonder if this really was his true calling.

Which brings him to where he is now, in a bar on the other side of town, and where he sees the psychic surgeon on TV. He comes here sometimes, just to be where nobody knows him and nobody wants anything from him, plus for the excellent salted fish. Inevitably the other customers notice the stranger (their gaze always snags on his good looks and damaged eye), but they don't stare. Ambrosio is not used to blending in, to keeping a low profile, but here it seems right, for here, by withdrawing a little, by presenting the illusion of relative normality, just for a while, he protects those aspects of himself that are the most precious. Here, he has his gifts, but he keeps them hidden. Once the broadcast is over, some of the customers talk among themselves, some convinced, others not, and nobody asks him for his opinion. But we know what he is thinking. He is thinking, *That doesn't look so hard.*

And that night, in the bed of his lover, once a customer (she is one of the more persistent ones), he thinks it still. How simple it looked. His lover is lying naked on her back, this young woman whose first question about when she will find a husband has still not been properly answered, while her second, about when she will be blessed with a child, almost certainly has. That, he suspects, is why she is so reluctant to let go of him. Though there is no sign of it yet, no swelling of her tiny, taut belly with its golden hairs, he does suspect. He massages her breasts; she smiles. He kisses her navel, lays his hands over her stomach, keeps them there a while, then presses gently, as gently as a kitten working at its mother's teat. And she lets him. She lets him until he presses a little too hard, too deep, and she can feel his fingernails digging into her. Now it is no longer pleasant; it even hurts a little. She tries to push his hands away, and when that doesn't work she sits up and asks him what the hell he thinks he's doing. To which Ambrosio can only shrug and reply that he is doing nothing – nothing at all.

11

Parihaka

Parihaka, New Zealand, 1881

When they came for you, you held out your hands to receive the manacles, allowed them to slip over your wrists and be locked in place. Words failing them, your captors fixed you with a scornful glare, and you glared back. Then they turned and led you away. Three of your number followed, single file, straight-backed, through the mud and beyond the village boundaries, the very boundaries you had tried to maintain. Those men who'd arrested you, by contrast, were slack-footed, slouching, insubstantial and unwholesome, deficient in their feigned unity. This is how Hape tells it, at least. He says they knew you were the better man, and if they did not know it in their minds then they knew it at least in their bodies, for it was in their bodies that it showed.

He was there too. You never knew it, how he had followed you out to the perimeter where the arrests would take place, had crouched at some twelve or so yards behind a bush, as you and your companions began to fix the fence that had been pulled up the night before. Pointlessly, of course, because that was how it worked: the villagers put up the fence, the constabulary pulled it out again. It was ritual of a kind, predictable in its civility, but now it was coming to an end.

Hape is certain he knew they were coming before you did. Such are his senses so finely attuned. Crouched close to the earth, the tread of their boots shuddered through his, a few seconds before you and yours perceived them. So he shuffled himself nearer to the ground, like a burrowing creature, so as not to be seen by those motley Queen's men. Not to avoid arrest, you see, but rather not to be dragged out into the open, so that you would know he had been hiding there, watching you. And what would you have thought of that?

A year's sentence meant a year's absence. During that time, life in Parihaka went on as it had before: the fields were ploughed, seeds sown, the maize and tobacco harvested (it was a good year) and expeditions launched – some villagers were sent inland to collect bush food, others to the coast to gather what the sea could spare. The women collected the cobs that had been fermenting in the creek, plucked the chickens and disappeared into the cooking huts, from which thick and fragrant smoke rose, a sign of the chemistry inside. The children scooped up the husks and feathers and dirt in their small hands and made them into playthings. Nothing was wasted. Order was the order of the day. At dusk the streets were swept clean, and they stayed so into the night, until long before sunrise, when baking smells stirred the villagers in their beds. A sweetness ascending, and the streetlights that had watched over Parihaka the night through yielded their duty to the new day.

Over all this the Prophets presided. Well – the Prophets – that is what they were called, although I fail to see the prophetic wisdom of men who allowed what happened to happen. In any case, they were much respected – by you, by Hape, by all. They brought everyone together, reminded them of the laws upon which harmony was based. Not only the harmony of the village, but of humanity itself. I suppose those who did not respect its governing principles – of forbearance, love of God and the Brotherhood of Man – would not have stayed in Parihaka. There were, after all, plenty of other places a man might otherwise live, or die.

No wonder you all felt so protected, and loved. All of you except Hape. He went on too, dutifully following the rhythm of the days, weeks, seasons, even though your absence hurt him deeply. Terribly at first, and then closer to the time of your release, not so much. Because he knew that the years are links in a chain, and each is bound to the one before it.

And because he had decided to forget you. He could not entirely, of course, but I still admire his resolve, and am charmed by the youthful naivety that made him think it might be possible. He knew you did not want him – you had been so firm about that – and so he did not see the point of further longing. Hape was not fond of stoical suffering, though he'd been schooled to be. He thought over and over again about the moment you had gripped his arm, not to reciprocate his touch but to guide it away – to remove him as one does an animal that has wandered into the house, an animal that is merely harmless and pitiable, like a mouse or a lizard. That grip was forceful, shaming. It was the first time you had touched him and, Hape was sure, the last. When he heard you had volunteered to be in the next group of men to fix the fence and be arrested, to martyr yourself for Parihaka, his sorrow was weighed against his relief. You had rejected him. But please, do not misunderstand. Hape did not wish you to be punished for that; it was only that your removal seemed to offer a resolution to his pain. He watched you leave, your muscle and sinew garlanded in iron, and then he trod back through the bed of damp earth and leaves to his plot, and to the gentle bleating of his goats, to live a simple life inured, he hoped, to such desires.

I have heard the story of your return more than once. The first time I did not want to hear it; nor, I admit, did I the second. Not even the third. It took me many years to understand why Hape insisted on repeating it to me. Well, now that I do understand, I do not mind telling it myself.

An autumn day. There had been showers that morning, but only briefly so the streets were not too muddied. The rain had plucked at the earth and unleashed the scent of it, and it mingled with the sweetness of the bread and the flowers that had been gathered and strewn in welcome across the marae. You must have noticed them, for when you arrived, with the forty-seven other released men, your face was tilted to the ground. You trudged to the marae, then stood, stooped, in your place. This made you difficult to find among the men. At first he thought you weren't there, but then, yes, unmistakably there you were. The crowd was jubilant, yet throughout all the welcoming ceremony you didn't once look up. You seemed to be trying to hide yourself.

That expression – a broken man – it comes to me now. Because in Hape's retelling you did not raise your head to recognise the world that had assembled to greet you. I don't mean the families gathered with yours, nor the women twirling their poi, the children singing, the men performing haka, the Prophets making their speeches and revelling in what they cast as the triumph of your return. Rather I mean the substance of the world – the fragrant, fleshy pines, the flash of bird-wing, the mountain petering out into the rich earth beneath you. Was it not different to the ground you had trod on in your captivity? Did you not notice this? When they beat you, had you not fallen into unknown soil? And now, here, what you were standing on was the earth of your own land, and though your body was bent towards it, you seemed to have forgotten your connection to it. A kind of amnesia. The whole village was alive and joyful, but you – your memories and emotions seemed to be dragging behind that body of yours, like the entrails of something wounded.

I suppose for you the transformation was slow. It began in that very first hour, when the manacles pulled at your wrists, bruising your skin. This, only the first of bodily humiliations, was to prepare you for the hard labour that your sentence dictated. What you men endured most in the village would come to know: the darkness and dankness of the big ships that bundled you as far as the south island, an imprisonment worse than you could have imagined, for the bad air got into you at once, and before long your shackled ankles ached, they seemed to be swelling, but all of this would have been bearable if you did not feel your spirit aching alongside, for your spirit was the only thing that might prop up your body, and without it they were both doomed. The voices around you trembled, 'Let us be strong, we will return in a year, a year in a life is nothing, a year will pass quickly' – but nobody believed it.

You spent most of the journey folded into a position from which it would be difficult to unfold again. Hape says that you never did entirely. By the time you arrived in Otago Harbour, the ache was part of you. It was your woe throughout the day, lay close beside you at night and was there too when you woke, all crumpled up and stale, as if it had rolled and shifted with you in the darkness. And when you hauled the stones that would cobble the streets of Dunedin, or talked back to your captors, it flared slightly in place of an anger you could not articulate. A knock here, a kick there, they forged you into a new shape and in time you did not notice it any more, for it seemed a natural companion to your labour, as inevitable as the process of living.

I know that pain makes one small, and that the only thing one can do, when there is no refuge, is to contract into oneself, to be tiny and hard. For a pebble will survive anything.

Before your arrest it had not been love. For love needs a small spark to begin, a touch or a glance, the smallest sign of acknowledgement, and you gave him none of these.

Hape was merely one of many village boys from a family you did not know, whom you had no business to know, whom you did not care to know. The beauty of your body, sculpted and turned by God and by toil, confounded him. His throat felt perpetually dry, yet no amount of water would help. He suffered and did not know the reason, only perceived it as a cruelty that had been visited upon him. Yet it was one he would not have forsaken. The Prophets had taught him forbearance; he knew no other path. Till one day, when from nowhere at all and quite by accident (for no one could have designed such an encounter) you brushed past him, and his cross fell from his shoulders. You said, 'I beg your pardon,' and Hape stammered his reply, reaching out and laying his hand upon your forearm (such impudence!), partly in an innocent impulse of brotherly concern, partly in a calculated move to stop you moving on, partly because he could do nothing else; and that was when he caught the spark. Such a tiny, involuntary gesture on your part, but it was enough. His grip tightened around your arm and he whispered, 'Please,' and you looked back down at him, confused but uncaring. 'Please what?' and Hape saying, 'I need – you,' and whether you understood him fully or not you shook yourself free and whispered back fiercely, looking him in the eye, 'Boy, you are mistaken in your needs. Need God.' And you walked away, leaving him there, feeling something new, but not knowing what – not yet.

That came after you returned. He was still young then, but he felt himself much older. He imagined that what had happened with you had been a test from the Lord. Nobody had seized his soul as you had. He conceived it as an involuntary madness, a tic or a spasm, the remnants of immaturity before a man learns how to master his emotions. Right up until the day of your return he was sure he had triumphed, and at the welcoming party he deliberately put himself at the front of it, to come face to face with you and to delight in the steadfastness of his character. But, oh, when he saw you like that, so diminished, so weak, how he crumbled. And how glad I am that he did.

He is sleeping now, my Hape. He is in bed. No, the two things are not always twinned. Sometimes he will fall asleep at his workbench; he lays his head on the thatch of his arms, always intending that it be for only a minute, but then he is away. Later I will find him, turn off the lamp that is warming his head and take him to bed, as he has told me I must. He doesn't like to wake up and find I am not there. But tonight he has fallen asleep beside me. Tonight we drank together – it was my birthday, so he could be persuaded – do you disapprove? Then he nestled into me, into sleep.

And I am awake, listening in the dark to his breath, and to the crackling above us as the tin roof cools. My arm is hurting; this has superseded the pleasure of having him there, so I pull it out from under his head; he stirs, and I repositioned myself to curl around him. I hope we will stay like this all night, so that when he wakes he knows he is at home. But for that I would need to fall asleep now too, and I don't think I can. I am wide awake, thinking about you, whom I will never meet, and yet how everything I know about you leads to me.

That is how it is. I am awake because of an unpayable debt. Because it was from you that my Hape learnt compassion, and with you that he learnt love. Forgive me – I have so richly profited from your misfortune, but so great is my joy, if it could be undone now I would not let it.

Everyone pretended that the return of the fencers was an ordinary thing – part of the cycle of life at Parihaka. Men resisted, they were arrested (calm in their shackles, shaming their oppressors) and later they returned (proud in their freedom, virtuous in their forbearance), and went back to their homes, where their children were a little taller, their women a little more tired. You too pretended that your homecoming was something ordinary. You returned to your family and tried to start again, to become part of that which you had left. But you could not. Your body would not allow it. Simple tasks could not be fulfilled. Your arm, which had been broken, was healing badly. Even to dress yourself was a trial. So your wife unstitched your shirts and added to them a band of material so that you could manoeuvre your arm in. Your youngest son helped you with this, then would follow you around, in case you needed help again. In your baggy white smock you looked like a ghost that had limped in from the past.

Yes, I know about this, too. Hape has told me how he approached your home some weeks after your return. How he walked down through the rows of houses, the smoky air and the stillness of winter, with no other purpose than to be nearer to you. He told me: he had not for a second intended to knock at your door or speak to you, but before he knew it he'd rounded the corner, and your house was in full view, and at that very same moment you stepped out of the door and paused there, perfectly embedded in the tranquillity. Hape's eyes were well trained now to track you from afar, as one does a bird in foliage. No sudden movements. Not wanting to be seen, Hape slowed his gait, then slunk into a space between two houses.

His breathing slowed, his gaze was steady. You were moving with difficulty but moving nonetheless – picking up and dragging branches from one side of your land to the other. Frequently you stopped to rest, and in those moments you kneeled in the ground, in the dirt, and because of the angle of your body your face was obscured from him.

Back and forth you went, resting in between. Upon your fourth pause, Hape became worried. You had become so very still, like a timepiece that has not been wound. And so very far in the distance. Your head to the ground. Hape advanced a few metres and suddenly you stirred, your head lifted and turned and you called back into the house. Out came your son, who took your instructions and disappeared inside again. When he returned he was holding a coat. Of course you must have been getting cold out there, your exertions were too feeble to warm the body – how could Hape have not perceived that? Haltingly you stood (you must know it was a pitiful sight) as your son, less than half your size, tried valiantly to lift your coat over your shoulders and to guide you into it. It seemed an impossible feat. You grimaced as the boy tugged at your coat, tugged at you, trying to bring the two together and all the time your face strained, exhausted, the breath billowing from it. Hape stood back, realising you were getting colder and colder out there, anxious that even if your son did succeed in dressing you, you might still freeze to death.

So immersed was he in your struggle he did not imagine that when your son went back inside you might at once look up in his direction and see him hiding there. Oh, the shame of it! You saw him, and in doing so you gave him no choice but to come out into the open.

You greeted each other like men, with no recognition of what had once passed between you. Hape asked what you were doing outside, and you replied that you were preparing to chop wood. Hape, without another word – for he had already exhausted his small stock – went and took your axe and positioned a log and struck it, splitting it in two, then in four. He put another on the block and continued the work. He expected you to rise, to insist you could manage, but you did not. You sat there shivering and over the course of nearly an hour let him chop the lot, so that by the end of it Hape was standing wet with perspiration and you were hunched, cold and tight. When all was done, you had your wife feed him, and she did so calmly and without betraying any thoughts on the matter. After that Hape would return every few days to help with your chores, and you would sit outside with him, though you did not have to, though you might have gone inside and observed him from the window instead, as your wife and son did with curiosity once in a while.

Everyone thought that Hape was such a good lad, so much did his neighbourly charity exceed all expectations. I am sure that he was. But what they did not know was how much he gained in return. Helping you changed him utterly. And this transformation – from desire to pity, to affection, to love – seemed to him as natural and logical as the turning of the seasons. His emotions could not have been ordered any other way. So that by the time winter was over, Hape was so brimming with love that he would have done anything for you, had you asked. He did not tell you this but you must have known it. A man must know.

You tolerated it, perhaps, because you knew the world was coming to an end. Hape says he was probably the only person in Parihaka who was not aware of it, but looking back the signs were clear: the ever more forceful petitions to stop ploughing and fencing, the swelling of government agents at the village boundaries – they stood watching, waiting for nightfall. The Prophets called their flock together more often, and more urgently. It was an acceleration towards a collective fate that neither you nor Hape would evade. Invasion was imminent. And then the village leaders decreed that the fences protecting it should be dismantled – the military would come anyway, why let them destroy more than need be? And the good people of Parihaka were instructed to ready themselves, to gather on the marae in peace and to receive the invader with open hearts.

And here Hape lost you. He was summoned back to his family and went with his father to the marae. His mother had joined the women baking bread for the invaders; his younger sister had gone to the village gates to sing for them. And where were you? You should have been on the marae too, but Hape could not find you there. He sat still, straining his head above the assembly; he did not dare to do more. He wondered – he still does – if you could hear the welcoming song of the children, the sign that Parihaka was surrounded by hundreds of armed constabulary men and twice as many civilians, volunteers hoping to get a piece of land for their troubles. The gathering was defined by the dread of what was to take place, but Hape's fear was different – it came from not knowing. As the night wore on the invaders held off outside the village boundaries, and, inside them, those whose fear was surpassed by exhaustion began to slump over the laps of their kin.

When they finally came, Hape stirred. He had fallen asleep; his father had let him. He had the urge to jump up, to run through the crowd and find you, but as everyone remained sitting he too had to stay where he was. The horses came, their hooves kneading the earth. So many of the villagers were visibly distressed. Hape's father and mother held his hands – they had not done this for a long time. They bound him back to them. The invaders surrounded. Hearts thumped in terror. Everyone prayed as they waited for the scale of the destruction to reveal itself.

I was twelve when Parihaka was destroyed. Though I had grown up far away, I'd heard about the village before then – with its stubborn, charismatic leaders, how they had held on for so long, those troublemakers who insisted Crown land was their own. I cannot say, at that age, that I had an opinion about it one way or the other – perhaps this was because my parents did not, for they already had their plot and were not much troubled by what lay beyond it. It was a distant conflict among parties who bore no relation to us. From time to time we witnessed native prisoners, sentenced to hard labour, toiling on the streets of our city, but they came from many places, and I did not associate them with the stories of the rebellions in the north. I did not feel sorry for these men; they were less than a curiosity to me. You see, I myself still had much to learn about compassion.

In any case my path would not have crossed yours. You were working on the roads of another city. But my imagination is not very great, and when Hape first told me about you I immediately thought of those men I had seen long ago – shackled, chipping at stones and laying them into the ground. Since I did not remember a single one of their faces, my memory plucked some dark-skinned stranger out from them, for he was an older man, and slowly Hape's descriptions fell upon him, transforming him into something human – into you. Your name was Ahiahi. You had large, black, watery eyes that turned up at the tear ducts, like smiles. A single white hair grew from the crest of your left ear, and along the length of your right arm ran a pink scar. When you spoke your tongue flickered behind a split front tooth.

Strange, I realise now, that Hape has never said whether these were there before your capture. I could ask, but I don't think I ever will. It still hurts me when he talks about you, and he knows this, so he has not done it in a long while. Perhaps he is restraining himself; perhaps he no longer feels the need. But I catch myself watching him and am aware that I cannot know the moments in which you are present. I'm watching him now, in the dark. This time it is I who have invoked you. Of course, these were only small observations of his. Hape never achieved the closeness that a lover does – the smell of you in the morning, the weight and the pull of you, the sounds of your slumber.

It took a fortnight to destroy Parihaka. To evict the visitors, to plough up the marae, plunder the houses and tear up the fields. To make it completely uninhabitable. Hape's family collected what remained of their belongings and left, and it all happened in a hurry, there were so few farewells. Hape lost you and, I think, you lost him. But in your frailty he gained something great, and so have I. When I think about you now, above all else it is with gratitude. For his tenderness, which is everything I have.

12

Salam

Aïn Oussara, Algeria, 1988

Sitting on the floor in his underpants, Karim Abdulchaou surveyed his surroundings. Rough white walls, floor and ceiling, each about four metres square – a perfect cube of empty space. A window had been cut out of one wall, a doorway from another. The window was covered with a square piece of red fringed cloth that filtered the sun's blaze into pink; in the frame of the doorway hung a curtain of plastic beads in opaque orange and white, which swooshed and swayed in a light, merciful breeze.

Next he turned his attention to his body, as anyone in this situation is bound to do. As he sat with his legs crossed, his gaze was drawn first to the callused soles of his feet and his hairy thighs. He examined his hands, which were resting in the basket of his legs. Then he clenched his fists, and the tendons and muscles in his arms rose to the command. They looked good and strong, and they led to a good and strong torso, too. Karim was, however, slouching. *Sit up straight!* he told himself. An old lesson, easily forgotten. Sometimes when he sat upright it caused a twinge of pain, but overall it made him feel better, and with his broad shoulders held back and abdomen firm, you could see what fine shape he was in. It was because he was prideful, and took care of himself. He had an image to maintain and did not want anyone saying he had aged badly.

He looked strong, but more importantly, he looked employable. When he had presented himself at the foreman's office, with his superb posture and powerful arms, and he'd reeled off the list of things he had done and those that he could do, why would they not believe him? So Karim Abdulchaou found himself hired immediately to work on the new construction site outside of town, the one that was a bit hush-hush.

The site must have been established a while, as the clearing and surveying had already been carried out and the building phase had begun. It was full of Chinese men, all wearing yellow hard hats and orange vests. Everything looked very orderly. 'The Chinese are helping us with this build,' the foreman told him. 'You don't mind them, do you?' Karim did not know if he minded Chinese or not – he hadn't seen many before and had certainly never spoken to one – anyway, whether he minded or not was beside the point. He needed the work and would have given the same answer regardless. Of course he didn't mind. Honestly, though, he didn't realise how many of them there would be. Scanning the site, he estimated that the locals were outnumbered two to one, and the Chinese even had their own separate hierarchy of workers, but somehow the whole thing seemed to run smoothly.

A fortnight later, Karim collapsed under the weight of a metal coil he had been carrying over one shoulder. Although not trapped beneath it, he could not get up again – he'd just tipped over, like a wheel falling off a cart. Two Chinese workers came over to help but could not get him to stand and, unable to communicate with him, they quickly gave up and went off to find a local. The Algerian they brought back was called Ali, a small but brawny man, who by crouching in the dust beside him reminded Karim of some kind of insect.

'Old injury,' Karim explained, glancing sideways up at Ali. 'Sometimes gets the better of me.'

'Very old injury?' Ali said.

'Very old.'

'I see.'

The Chinese workers had resumed activity around them. Ali let Karim rest for a few minutes, then helped him up and sat with him while he sipped at a lukewarm, sugary tea. Yes, it happened during the revolution. Yes, he had tried all kinds of treatment. The tea soothed his dry throat but not the shooting pain in his back; talking about it always made it worse, it got him all worked up inside. He could feel things tightening up again. There were tears in there too, somehow contained, but not in a way he had any control over. Imagine, the great Karim Abdulchaou bursting into tears after a fall! He didn't know Ali, didn't know if he could trust him to keep a thing like that to himself. And yet he felt so delicate, like something that might break with the slightest touch. He had felt like this before, but he had always recovered, even if sometimes it had taken a while. God was truly watching over him.

So was Ali. Watching him intently, waiting for those tears. 'Do you know what a Chinese would do in your place?' he said. 'They would go to their own doctor. Apparently they work miracles. The men here have one they go to, in the town; they brought him along with them. If you like I could try to get you in. And,' he went on, 'they're cheap. Really cheap. Like only half of what you'd expect.'

Well, that was something.

'What do you say then? What have you got to lose?'

In the white room Karim could hear the nervous quiver of a distant radio, as the wind sent the sound this way and that. A car radio, he thought. The beaded curtain clattered gently, and the light coming in through the curtains rippled and beat onto the wall. Then came a pair of sounds that did not dance back and forth with the rest, but were as firm as the footfall that accompanied them. Steadily they grew more audible. Karim got to his feet. Voices. The two were coming back, having instructed him some minutes ago to remove his outer clothes and 'wait restfully' while they were gone. The interpreter entered first, a lanky half-Chinese, half-something-else man called Nestor who spoke fluent French and a bit of Arabic, and was the main interpreter on the site; he was followed by the doctor Zhang Tengfei, in his thirties with a smooth, high forehead and straight black hair pulled back into a brush-like ponytail, giving his head a comfortingly sanitary appearance. The doctor spoke.

'He says you should sit down,' said the interpreter. 'He says you should relax.'

Karim suddenly became aware of his clothes discarded, like a shed skin, piled in the corner of the room.

'Maybe I could,' he said, lowering himself back down, 'if I didn't have to pay for an interpreter as well. I thought this was going to be cheap.'

The interpreter did not translate that. Instead he said, 'I'm afraid you cannot do without me, Mr Karim. But don't worry, I'm not expensive. You won't regret it.'

'I'd better not,' Karim muttered. The bother was making his back ache even more. Why he had no control over this simplest of mechanisms – his emotions – exasperated and tired him. He felt constantly on the verge of defeat.

'He is worth it,' the interpreter said, gesturing to the doctor. 'His father was a practitioner, his grandfather before him, and his great-grandfather before that.'

Well, Karim thought, *my father was a drunk and a traitor, so what's your point?* But he didn't say anything. The doctor seemed not to have noticed his irritation, or, at the very least, was ignoring it. He sat down on the mat across from Karim and invited the interpreter to do the same, so that the three of them made a rough triangle.

'Tell him about the nature of your complaint,' the interpreter said.

Karim obliged, then listened as the information, distorted by translation, made its way to the doctor.

'Now show him precisely where it hurts.'

Karim turned around, displaying his back to them, and the doctor and interpreter leaned in. He had some sense of what they were looking at – the places where the scar tissue had thatched over, the ridges and grooves across his shoulderblades. He felt the doctor's fingertips begin to move there, pressing lightly across his back like the soft tread of a cat. 'When it hurts, say.' Some spots were tender, some more so, while others were miraculously free from pain, as if they had ceased even to exist. Karim felt the doctor was mapping an invisible constellation across him, with some of the stars bright and more vivid, and others very far away, a mere glimmer. The rest, nothingness.

'So,' the interpreter said, 'an old injury. Old scars.'

'Yes.'

'From the time of the war?'

'Yes.'

'And you have been suffering all this time?'

Karim paused. *No, not all this time.* He wanted to tell them that for the most part he had led a good life, that there had been times of immense happiness. That he had experienced fortune and contentment. That he was grateful for that which he had gained, and for that which he had not lost: his home, his wife, his son, his honour. But the doctor would not be interested in those. Karim explained that the pain had steadily lessened over the years, and now mostly just flared up during physical activity or stress. Or when he thought or spoke about it, as he did now.

Zhang Tengfei responded with a murmur, almost quizzical, that Karim could not quite gauge.

'*Fàngsōng,*' the doctor whispered.

'Relax!' barked the interpreter. So Karim closed his eyes, and when that did not work, he stared at the ruffled shadow on the wall. There followed a long silence during which the interpreter did not move yet seemed also to withdraw. The doctor took Karim's hand, cupped it firmly in his own, his forefinger pressed into the pulse point. Then he took the other. When that was done he asked Karim questions about his sleep, diet and bowel movements, about which parts of him felt too hot and which too cold. He examined his eyes, then his tongue. While this was being done, Karim tried not to blink or breathe too heavily, and forced himself to sit up straight. Such an effort! By the end of it he felt quite fatigued.

Now, *hamdulillah*, it was time to lie down. Without another word the interpreter left the room – a rustle of the bead curtain and he was gone. Karim lay there, one side of his face pressed into the mat, and watched as the doctor busied himself in the corner. There was a clatter and a tinkle, the sound of instruments being prepared. Karim did not know what to expect. He felt his heart beat faster and heavier in his chest, and goosebumps broke out all over him. Though he knew there was no need to be scared, his poor body did not.

Coming to sit beside him the doctor unfolded on the ground a white sheet of paper, inside the creases of which lay several fine needles. He held one up for Karim to see – a delicate thing that reminded him of the proboscis of a mosquito. Then between his shoulderblades Karim felt the pressure of fingers, a flicking sound and a pinching sensation. He felt the needle being manipulated deeper, and the area became briefly infused with a sharp pain. *Fàngsōng!* Before Karim had the chance to register what was happening the doctor had moved to the next spot, and was tapping a needle in there also. He seemed to remember precisely each point at which Karim had registered the most pain and now he was returning to all of them, as well as to some Karim had not mentioned – across his back, neck and shoulders, hands and legs. Having finished inserting the needles he jostled all of them once more, sending small measures of discomforting heat down each one. *Fàngsōng*, he counselled again, then padded out of the room.

Now Karim was alone in there once more. He lay still, waiting for the doctor to return, but the seconds stretched into minutes and then those minutes doubled, and eventually he lost all sense of how much time had passed.

He was lying crab-like, his arms bent near his head. Cautiously he tried to raise himself up onto his elbows, but he did not get very far because it made all the needles in him shift too, sprinkling a fine pain across him. The only needle he could actually see was the one in his right hand, nestled at the juncture of his thumb and index finger. It did not seem to be inserted very deeply, as it wobbled unsteadily when he flexed his hand. The ones in his back seemed more firmly embedded, and he feared that if he moved too much they might even snap off in him. And so he lowered his head back down onto the mat, and resigned himself to his fate.

His mind wandered for a while before it settled in the place it inevitably must – the room in the police station where they had tortured him and his friends. It had happened early in the revolution, when they were all still very young and everything was slightly out of control. Karim was grateful that over time his memory had distilled those forty-eight or so hours, to produce not a uniform narrative of his degradation, but a series of static images around which one actively had to rebuild the sequence of events. He did not want to rebuild it. It was like looking at old photographs that prompt the recollection only of the moment the image was taken, rather than the event itself. Now, at the age of forty-six, he did not even remember the anger he felt afterwards, but he must have felt it, and deeply too, because immediately afterwards he'd joined the FLN, the National Liberation Front. They'd taken him in, given him the opportunity to retrieve his life and to avenge himself, and he had carried out the mission perfectly: a bombing of the entrance of the very station in which he'd been held. It had claimed two lives and injured several more. There was another mission after that too – a stabbing in the street – which had also gone fairly smoothly, much more so than he might have expected. And then the rest seemed to happen very quickly: the crackdown on the revolutionaries, the reprisals, the shift in fortune, the retreat of the French. Victory celebrations in the streets and across the nation, risen anew from the ashes of colonialism, and none of it – the plotting, the viciousness, the desperation – none of it was needed any more. For his role in the liberation of his country, for his martyrdom and heroism, Karim became, at the age of nineteen, a local hero. A month later his wife gave birth to their only son.

The intervening years offered nothing much to speak of. He worked in various construction jobs, co-owned a scrap metal dealership for a while. Watched his son grow up and his wife out. Sometimes the pain would get to him, and then he would lie down with a packet of cigarettes and work his way slowly through them, and there was some relief in that. Drugs he had tried years ago; they did not work well enough to justify the expense. Now he was working in the mountains for the government with a load of Chinese, and it was a promotion of sorts, if only he could stay upright. Working on what, it was none of his business.

The room was warm and had become gloomy, as though his settling thoughts were a fine dust falling through the air. Could it be that so much time had elapsed? It was impossible to tell. The close white walls with the corrugated pink light disoriented him. He felt heavy, and then, he felt nothing.

The next thing he knew the doctor was sitting beside him. Karim had not even heard him come in. He lifted his head slightly and realised that he must have fallen asleep, for a spool of saliva had collected at the corner of his mouth and dribbled out onto the mat. Embarrassed, he went to wipe his mouth but could not move his arms. Zhang Tengfei quickly cupped a cloth beneath it, patting it dry as one does a baby's. 'Ça va, ça va,' the doctor said.

'Merci,' Karim stuttered in reply, but it was evident that this was the only French phrase the doctor knew. Karim suspected that the interpreter had taught it to him in the time that had passed. Groggily, he tried to rouse himself while the doctor removed the needles and set about ener-getically massaging his back and legs. He worked upon Karim as if he were a raw material to be moulded, and when that was done, his movements became more gentle, even soothing. He sealed his handiwork by covering his patient's back in a strong camphoric liquid, rubbed it briskly in, and ended by slapping his shoulder: 'Ça va!'

On the way home Karim stopped at the *hammam*. He'd had enough of being undressed and manipulated, but he stank of the strange substance and did not want to have to explain it to his wife. He didn't want to talk about any of it – not what had happened at work, and certainly not the necessity of having to spend money on oriental medicine. Yet while the *hammam* cleansed his body of the stuff, it had also infused his clothes, and as soon as he walked in the door his son – who lived with them along with his son's wife – remarked on the smell.

'God, what's that stench? What kind of nasty chemicals have they got you working with up there, Baba?'

Fortunately, his wife and daughter-in-law were out. Karim peeled off his shirt, threw the offending item into a tub of water, and returned to his son. Now he was bare-chested, but the smell stayed on him nonetheless.

'Don't tell your mother, but I went to see a doctor today, for my back. A Chinese one. It's been bad lately, I had to try something new. Don't tell her, it will only worry her.'

'Well, now *I'm* worried,' said his son. 'So you are working for the Chinese and you're giving them your business too!'

'Not working for them,' Karim sighed, 'working *with* them. I work for the government. There are only a few Chinese,' he added. He knew what Samy thought of the Chinese – that they were modern-day imperialists, capitalists under the veneer of socialism, feigning international friendship while they sucked the continent dry. Samy said that the Es Salam reactor wasn't about enriching the nation or helping it to stand on its own two feet. Cheap energy now, he was fond of saying, but they would pay for it later.

'Did it work at least? This voodoo?'

Not responding immediately made him look uncertain, but until that moment Karim had not actually taken stock of how he felt after the treatment. His body was like a new coat that could only be properly judged in front of a mirror – he needed a moment to inhabit it thoughtfully, to consider it from all angles and with greater attention than usual. Somehow he did feel different. He might not be able to say he was cured exactly, but perhaps the nature of his discomfort had shifted somehow. He did feel more relaxed, and so the pain in his back that had troubled him earlier seemed to have dulled, yet he also felt overcome with a great exhaustion and sadness, a hollowing-out. This he had not noticed after the acupuncture or even while being pummelled at the *hammam*. But now, standing here in his own home, in front of his son, he suddenly felt that he was about to collapse.

'It did, I think. I think it takes a while to work properly. A few treatments.'

'Uh-huh.' His son nodded incredulously. 'Well, you look fucking terrible. I'd ask for my money back if I were you.'

'You won't tell your mother?'

'Baba, I'll be happy to keep your secret. I wouldn't like to upset my dear old mum. But then again, if I hear that you've become too fond of the place, I might have to review our confidentiality clause.'

It was not the time, then, for Karim to mention that he'd already decided he would go back. He went to lie down, his second nap for the day. Maybe this was his natural state? At that moment he felt that being anything other than perfectly horizontal was unnatural, a kind of self-deception. He lay there, hoping to drift off again in the precious minutes he had to himself, before the women got back and started fussing over him, but he could not. Instead he worried about his son. An educated boy. Why so disrespectful? Where had he learnt such language? Had he no shame? What did he have against the Chinese? They were hard workers, trying to help. Unlike Samy, who barely lifted a finger. He complained about things, yet did nothing about them. Karim loved his son, but he was not proud of him; he often regretted that he had not had a better one. But then he was lucky to have any children at all. God bless Samy. He wasn't perfect, but he was all they had. Perhaps one day his son would change. It was possible; such things were not unknown.

Those thoughts loosened up the tears that until then had remained safely stored inside him. Released after so long, they ran in great streams. Karim turned on his side, buried his face into the mattress, breathed in the remnants of the camphoric liniment that still clung to him somehow, somewhere, and slipped into a deep sleep.

The next time he visited the doctor, the interpreter was nowhere to be seen. Karim waited outside for five minutes before Zhang Tengfei poked his head outside to summon him in.

'*Bonjour*,' Karim greeted him.

'*Bonjour!*' he replied cheerily, bowing a little. '*Ça va, ça va*,' the doctor added, ushering him in. Evidently he was in a hurry to begin. Karim sat down as he knew he should. '*Fàngsōng, fàngsōng*,' the doctor chimed. Karim breathed in deeply, looked at the mat. The doctor beckoned him to hold out his hand, and he knew it would be cold to the touch. The doctor took it loosely and exclaimed, then mimed a shiver. *Cold like last time!* They both smiled. He counted Karim's pulse, the smile still on his lips, and by the time he had returned his hand to him and taken the other it had faded into a pursed concentration.

In from the sun the interpreter came, so frazzled and apologetic that he barely noticed they had begun without him. The doctor ignored him until he had finished his internal counting, then chastised him; the interpreter seemed, to Karim, surprisingly wounded. He sat penitent a metre further away from them than he had before, and sipped from a glass of water while he listened to the advice he was about to relate.

'Mr Karim, let me explain what is wrong with you. Perhaps you think you know already, and it is very simple – you were injured once, and the pain will not go. That is so, but it is only part of the story. You suffered a traumatic injury. But why does your body not heal after so many years? If you cut yourself, the body heals, right? You are not very old, you are not feeble, so we ask, why does it not heal now? The answer is your qi. This is your energy pathway. Not blood or air or electricity, something else, but connected. Remember that everything is connected. Your qi is deficient, it is stagnating – that is the problem. So your blood is stagnant. And because it will not move as it should, new blood cannot be generated. Your hands are cold because your blood is cold. There is no harmony inside you; you have internal imbalance. That is why you are unwell. This malignant blood. That is why you have no vitality in your eyes. But do not worry, I will help you.'

And with that Zhang Tengfei dismissed the interpreter who, still perspiring, obediently slunk back outside, empty glass in hand. Then he motioned Karim to lie down.

Out of balance, Karim thought as the doctor shuffled around his body, tapping the tiny needles into him. *Disharmonious. Stagnant. Deficient.* Karim pictured a pool of reeking, dirty water, in which all the muck had sunk to the bottom, leaving only the larvae of some parasitic creature to breed happily on the surface. He could not help but feel a little insulted.

Above him, the doctor was speaking – seemingly to him, but perhaps only to himself. His tone was lively and engaged – even, Karim fancied, optimistic. When he finished, he offered his customary *ça va* and stood to leave again.

'*Ça va, merci,*' Karim replied, but too late, for he had already gone.

Once again he had been left there to think. He imagined the blood in him sinking towards the floor, as in a mud-filled pond, as in a dead thing. But no – he stopped himself – wasn't his imagination deficient too? Because what these needles were doing, though he could not feel it, was drawing blood to them, stimulating it, moving it around him. They were conductors of energy. Perhaps when the doctor touched the needles he sent his own energy down them too. Did the man have it to spare? Or did the needles draw warmth from the air and into him? Karim clenched his fist, the hand with the needle in it, and delighted in the stab of pain at that point. Tenderness, he now knew, meant the right spot; tenderness meant it was working. Suddenly he felt lighter, more hopeful.

Yes, this was something new, something the doctor had given to him.

So many years, Karim considered wistfully, to be deficient. He thought back to those days in custody. The repeated shocks, the beatings. Two ribs broken, a dislocated shoulder, mouth like a smashed pomegranate. It had taken him several months to recover, but recover he had, and he'd been able to hold his newborn son without too much pain or difficulty. He'd returned to work and was active in the Front too. He'd been scarred but was not fearful. Perhaps it was the stupid courage of the young, but all had seemed to work out in the end. He got his vengeance. Algeria was liberated. He was a good man; he took care of his family, he did not lie or cheat, he was observant. All was as it should be. Except for this pain that returned to him, time and time again, long after the struggle was over. An inconsistency somewhere, something that had slipped beneath him and thrown him off balance.

There was only the one thing – he would say if pressed – that had always bothered him slightly. That gendarme he'd stabbed in the street. The Frenchman had been quite young, about the same age as Karim back then. The knife had slid into him like a whisper, and as the man fell to the ground he'd grabbed tightly onto Karim's wrist. Karim had promptly shaken him off and stomped on the wounded man's hand. Then he'd kicked him in the jaw and fled the scene. If anybody prompted him – although no one ever had – Karim would say that he had always felt this to be an ignoble gesture on his part. It would not have been difficult to release the young man's grip with his hand, to simply let him fall to the ground and to leave. Crushing and kicking him had not been necessary. It was thuggish, how he'd handled it – immature. But *he* had been immature, and he had panicked. This was how Karim had always justified those actions to himself. He learnt later that the young Frenchman had survived; he was eventually discharged and sent back to his true homeland, a few years before the flood of his fellow *Pieds-Noirs*.

Perhaps *this* was it, then, the single event in his life that had caused all this disharmony in him – the pointlessness of this act, the wanton cruelty. Perhaps that was why he had never spoken about it to anyone. Wounding a man for no good reason, and perhaps this man, too, had suffered a long time from his injuries. Perhaps shame was at the root of his deficiency. Stagnant shame. Perhaps that was it.

While Karim was pondering all this, Zhang Tengfei came back in and crouched beside him, wordlessly manipulating the needles. Karim had stopped being aware of them, but the agitation brought them back to life. The doctor then gently pressed his fingers upon the surrounding tissue, spoke softly in Chinese and left the room again. Karim remembered the first time he had been left on his own in there, incapacitated, with no explanation and no sense of when anyone would return – how unnerving it had been. Now he found the absence soothing. He knew the doctor would return to tend to him in not so long, but in the time until then he could enjoy the freedom to wander among his thoughts. He liked that the work performed on him took some time, that he was compelled to lie there and think. It seemed a necessary part of the treatment, of the process of attaining harmony. His body was a machine more complex that he had understood before, and what had been done to him – he knew now – could not be undone so easily.

And from this, Karim Abdulchaou came to his final understanding. He had been wrong about everything. The problem was not that he had wounded that man in the way he did. It was rather the opposite. For when you considered the universal laws of balance, that act was in fact the one that made the *most* sense – the young Karim had been injured by the French; he in turn had injured a young Frenchman. No, it was the one before that, the bombing, that had upset the balance of his life. Two people had perished in that attack, and five had been hurt – even taking into account the damage done to his two friends, who had also been tortured, it was still many more than was required to counter the original offence. Worst of all, it was this act that had given Karim the status he'd enjoyed since. It was the bad faith with which all this burdened him that had created the perpetual disharmony that tormented him now.

So that was it, the root of the problem. He knew it for sure when Zhang Tengfei returned and retrieved the needles, and he felt the tension lift out of him. When his back was massaged he felt lighter and more supple – more youthful even. Karim exhaled deeply as the doctor took his hands and dug his thumbs into them, then shook them to make a ripple down the length of his arms, and they were made liquid. He had to admit, however, that his hands did still feel a little cool and tight. But was that so strange, when they were the very hands that had planted the bomb? Karim did not protest when he heard the doctor open the bottle of the pungent liniment and cover his back in it. It tingled cold upon his skin, then hot. And he thought how miraculous it was that such equilibrium might be achieved by such opposing elements.

Afterwards the doctor called the interpreter back in, and the two spoke between them.

'He wants to know if you will be coming back,' the interpreter sighed. 'He advises treatment weekly until the problem is resolved. He says that I am no longer required. Before I go, then, I should ask you, as my last service to you, if I should arrange another appointment?'

Karim nodded. He had decided it long ago. He would see Zhang Tengfei every week, until the Chinese left, or until he ran out of money.

'That might be a very long time,' the interpreter said. 'You will surely be cured by then.'

'Perhaps,' Karim replied. '*Inshallah*. But I will come anyway.'

'Very well.'

Having paid them both, and the interpreter for the last time, Karim straightened himself up, stepped out under the colourless sky and began to walk through the town. He was aware of the smell on him, but passed by the *hammam* without going in. No more slouching. No more dawdling. From now on he would go directly home.

13

A dream that cannot be recalled

Birobidzhan, USSR, 1936

It is the late summer of that year, and a spectacular thunderstorm breaks out over Birobidzhan. The dogs pull their heads in and slink away, but the town's people, they come out to see – even those who are normally frightened of such storms, because this one is different. This storm resembles the fabled epiphany of near-death, when calm overtakes us and we are resigned to our fate, while still beholden to the wonder of life and the simple awe of the terrestrial. The lightning splinters the sky not from top to bottom but from side to side, its stalks splitting and joining like something organic, creating jagged nets of light that tessellate the darkness and then fade, leaving a pink afterimage in their wake. So that after watching for a while you see the night crossed with ghost-light, like the inside of your eyelids after you have squeezed your eyes shut for a minute, then opened them again.

I am standing beneath it, gripping the hand of a man who is not my husband. The man who is my husband stands to the other side of me, holding my other hand. The smell of smoke is in the air, that usual smell that permeates the town on summer evenings, but tonight it is as if it comes from the atmosphere itself, as if the lightning has singed the sky.

I was born in Buenos Aires, where, for the earliest years of my childhood, the smell of smoke was the smell of the past. It was the burnt tobacco accumulated in my grandfather's fingertips, the coal in my grandmother's stove, the birch pyres of the *shtetls* of my ancestors whom they never stopped telling me about. The smell of smoke was the smell of the past – at least until it seeped into the present.

I was about eight, I think, when my father came home one day with his clothes ruined and blackened by ash. He'd been trying to defend a neighbour's home, but in doing so had been pushed into the inferno. Blood streamed down his face, and there was a long gash across his left cheek. He closed his eyes as my mother dabbed at it, but there was so much dirt and ash in the wound she could not get it all out, and so it healed up with the ash embedded inside. This made the scar more pronounced, raised instead of grooved, with a strange grey tinge to it. My father was not proud of his efforts, as no good had come of them. Though my mother tried in vain to remind us it had been a heroic act, his discontent only cultivated the impression of victimhood that had attached to him. His scar became a symbol not of bravery, but of defeat. I saw how unhappy it made my mother – how when he came in that day smelling of smoke her life, too, shifted in the wrong direction, and she must have known then that all her calculations about their future together were to be proved wrong. I loved my father, but hoped I would not marry a man like him.

I did, of course. I married Daniel, who used to tell me it was fate that had brought us together. Yes, it was fate, but I knew it to be a secondary one. I was destined to meet Daniel because I was first destined to meet his older brother. Rubén had been at one of the Bund meetings my friends and I used to go to in those days – they were as social as they were political, a good place to find a partner. Everyone noticed Rubén, not only for his good looks but because he was the only one whose face had a prominent scar across it. He noticed me too, because I was the only one who stared at him for longer than was polite. His scar was just like Papa's; it was even on the same side of his face. I continued staring as he came over – a coincidence like this trumped all etiquette – and Rubén introduced himself to me with a line he had clearly used before: 'In case you're wondering, the lion lost.' I didn't care. I explained myself, how I hadn't meant to be rude, but it was just so striking, how his scar resembled my father's. Rubén replied that it was never a good idea to go out with anybody who looked like a relative. 'Who knows, you might be my sister!' he said. I wouldn't have minded if I were.

We fell into each other easily, without guilt or reservation. He wasn't my first lover, but he was the first with whom there was no need to pursue, or invent, or conceal. I waited a long time for Rubén to propose to me – I was sure he was the man I would marry – but instead he retreated, slowly, as if I might not notice, until he disappeared almost completely. As a kind of compensation he offered me his younger brother, Daniel, whom he'd begun to send to the meetings in his place. I was scandalised that Rubén would do such a thing, but I took Daniel anyway, and punished him because of it, until it no longer satisfied me to do so. Until finally, out of guilt and perhaps fear, I accepted the offering. Daniel, who at least did not have the capacity to hurt me. Dear Daniel, my secondary fate.

Rubén had left me for another woman. I heard later that she was pregnant and there was no getting out of it, but I held out a small hope that he would be released from her somehow. That maybe she would tire of him. Or that her baby would die. It was a terrible thought, but I did not punish myself for it. Such things do happen. With Rubén's mistake then erased, he could put things right with me. Maybe fate would reveal itself to be on my side after all.

It did, but in a different way. I had my own child, a little boy we named Diego. For the first year Daniel and I and our unblemished new baby lived together in a kind of exhausted bliss. My temperament calmed; I was no longer filled with anger. And although there was still an ache inside me, a new kind of love had replaced the one that was gone, and I figured that this was a reasonable measure of contentment for a woman like me. At least, I knew it logically, for in my heart I was always holding out for something more.

But then, how could I not, when all people talked about was utopia? It came up at some point in every meeting – how and where to build a homeland for our people – and the Ashkenazi press was full of it, with different columnists

espousing the relative virtues of the competing socialist Zions: Palestine, Peru, British East Africa, Western
Australia…I thought it was crazy, all of it, but kept
quiet – I always learnt something from hearing about those
exotic places, and the conviction with which my friends
promoted their favourite wonderlands confirmed my sense
that for each person there was such a thing as multiple fates,
and some of these fates were scattered across the world,
merely waiting to be found. I had not felt drawn to any of
the places that had been discussed so far, but at some point
a new contender emerged – a region in the far eastern
corner of the USSR on the Manchurian border, which
Stalin had set aside just for Jews. There, its proponents
crowed, the utopia had already been born, a community
forged in labour and in hope. Our Argentine branch even
sent a delegation, which reported favourably upon its
return. That was the point at which Birobidzhan became
real to me – when I heard someone speak who had actually
been there, who had breathed its air, made the journey
back, and still lived. Unlike the other places, which
remained mere dots on a map, this one was connected to
us somehow. Daniel became suddenly enthusiastic. Until
then I had never considered leaving Buenos Aires and the
country to which my family had come. I was worried that
going would insult their spirits somehow, that it would be
a declaration that Argentina wasn't good enough for me,
or for my son. It would be implying they had made the
wrong decision. I told my husband this, that my ancestors
had found a safe place to prosper, to raise children, to be
part of the world, and who were we to disagree? But I also
knew what he would say in reply: 'Look at your father,

look what they did to him. Do you think he is part of their world? He isn't and neither are we. This isn't our place, and once in a while they will push us into the fire just to remind us of it.'

It was I who ought to have been talking like this, not Daniel. His people were Sephardim. They had come from Morocco in the middle of the last century; they'd been in Argentina twice as long as mine and were completely integrated. They didn't even speak Yiddish. This annoyed me and I threw it in his face. 'If anyone should be going to Birobidzhan it's me!' I said.

'So go!' he replied. 'And I'll come a bit later when you've calmed down.'

I was curious but unconvinced. Then one day I arrived home to find Rubén sitting at our kitchen table. Rubén, whom I had not seen since he'd turned up after the birth of my son to hold Diego's hand as though he was his own – though he wasn't. Daniel knew I would listen to his brother, and Rubén played his part very well. 'If you're asking me about Birobidzhan, sure, you should go. I'd leave tomorrow if I could. Only I've got a few things tied up here first. I don't see why you three don't, though. Get things set up over there, and then I'll come and join you just as soon as I can.' The other things he said, like 'What's stopping you? The sooner the better! It'll be an amazing adventure. There's no future here anyway. Don't you want a good life for your son?' – I had already heard from Daniel. But coming from Rubén they made more sense.

He did not mention the woman he'd left me for. I didn't dare to ask if he was planning to bring her too, and

I couldn't ask in front of Daniel, in any case. But it didn't much matter – I had already decided that if Rubén went then I would go as well, that with him I could do it. Six months later, in March 1933, Daniel and I took Diego and began the journey, with a group of twelve other Argentine Jews, to Stalin's Zion. Rubén promised to follow us out within the year.

It was done. We had brought our little boy to a town on a marshland where it raged wet and hot in summer and during the stone-dry winters dropped to below twenty. Much of Birobidzhan had already been established: there were roads and public buildings, and the communes branched far throughout the district. Our family and other newcomers were housed in tents while our new homes – dark log cabins, the forests reconstructed – could be built.

Before the settlers came the town was just a stop on the Trans-Siberian, the accidental centre of a region sparsely populated by Russian Cossacks and Korean rice farmers, as well as a smattering of Ukrainians and Poles. With this new wave, overwhelmingly from Eastern Europe, came Yiddish, the *mameloshn* – the mother tongue; it was the official language of the region and by the time we arrived was in wide use. This was hard for Daniel at first. He had no connection to the language, nor was he convinced it was the best one for the New Jew. So he did not trouble himself much trying to learn it, apart from a few stock phrases needed for daily life. At first he got around the problem by associating mainly with other Argentines but, this proving too difficult, he decided to put his efforts into Russian instead. He'd once tried learning it from a book, way back when he'd first discovered socialism, as had so many other youthful idealists in those days. This had been Rubén's idea – that both brothers would one day make a pilgrimage to Moscow, so they'd better be prepared. 'And now here I am!' Daniel said triumphantly, a volume of Pushkin in his hands, as we sat in our new hut with the summer rain pouring down all around us.

That was the first time I heard that Rubén spoke Russian. I hadn't known that about him, but then I didn't know much – we'd only ever spent ten, perhaps twelve afternoons together. But it gave me renewed hope that he would join us very soon.

Sometimes in the night Diego would wake and cry. He was four by then, but because he was sickly he seemed younger – for that is what illness does, it pushes us back into the fragility of infancy, while our actual age lets us look on in curiosity as we rediscover our bodily selves. That was why he cried, I think – not out of pain or discontent, but because he didn't know who or where he was. And I couldn't tell him. 'There, *tsigele*, there,' I said, for Yiddish was the language of my grandparents, and so of the cradle, and now it was the language of everything else too – of work, of commerce, of politics and leisure.

I had joined the town's newly established theatre troupe, but before our first performance Daniel decided he would not come. 'It'll be too hard for me to understand,' he said. I replied that he might simply enjoy the spectacle of it, so he did come in the end, but thereafter usually stayed at home. The theatre was not really for him, you see. He had his books. He worked hard on the land all day and in the evening he just wanted to sit quietly and read with his family around him. But if, after she had kicked off her boots and scrubbed the dirt off her hands, his wife wanted to go and enjoy herself, then that was okay with him.

Our second play a few months later was, like most of them would prove to be, set in a *shtetl*. I played the role of a peasant woman, while my fellow performers, who also pretended to be old-world Jews, actually were – most had come from small communities in Central and Eastern Europe, or cities like Lvov, Odessa and Bucharest. I had a good friend in the troupe for a while – Anna. She was from the Ukrainian lands, and because my family was also from there we used to joke that we were long-lost sisters. But Anna left Birobidzhan only a few months in, after her youngest daughter almost died of pneumonia. Without an ounce of regret she told me I ought to take my child and go as well. She had to say it.

Perhaps I would have, too – whisked Diego away from there – if only, despite his maladies, he were not such a happy child. When I was on stage I looked down at him, the only audience I played to. His rapt expression, his little body leaning forward on the seat and his puppet legs swinging beneath it. He came to every performance, and he understood everything.

While on stage I began to notice that Diego had made a friend. Not a boy of his own age, but a grown man who attended nearly every show and often sat beside him. One night I observed the two talking, and after curtain call hurried off to approach the stranger before he left. Yet he too had decided to meet me that evening, and he stayed sitting with Diego as the crowd dispersed. He was a wiry

Korean with clay-brown skin. When I approached them he stood politely, introduced himself and congratulated me, in Yiddish, on my performance. His name was Kim, and he had a long scar across the left side of his face.

I realised then that I had been looking out for men like him — like Rubén, like my father — ever since I left Argentina. I felt I ought to thank the Korean for keeping Diego company, and then take my son home, but I lingered. This man was the first sign I had come across in years, and if I did not speak to him now, how would I know what to do next?

I thanked him for his kindness; I said I hoped he had enjoyed the performance.

'Oh yes,' he replied, 'I enjoy all of them. I'm glad they opened this theatre. Until then this town was rather dull.'

I complimented him on his Yiddish.

'Well,' he shrugged, 'I've been here a long time.' Before that he was in Vladivostok. Before that in some other place I hadn't heard of. And before that somewhere near the border, fleeing the Japanese. 'That's sort of how I ended up here,' he said.

Embarrassed, or perhaps pained by the revelation — I couldn't tell — he crouched down to Diego, their faces level. I watched as my son toppled forward to embrace his new friend. Then he pulled back a little and ran his open palm across Kim's grooved face. With his hand still pressed there he turned quizzically to look at me.

'Like your grandpa, remember?' I said to him in Spanish.

'And uncle,' he added immediately.

I was surprised he even remembered Rubén, and it occurred to me then that my boy would grow up thinking such marks were absolutely normal. I explained to Kim that he reminded us of someone we knew. I could hardly admit he reminded us of two.

'In Argentina?' he asked.

'Yes,' I said. 'His uncle. He misses his uncle. But then you seem to have become a kind of substitute.' I'd meant it as a joke, to lighten the tone of our conversation, but in uttering those words I understood that I'd given up waiting for Rubén to come. Fate had sent me this marked man, the sign that Rubén was now a figure of my past, and of Diego's too. I apologised to the Korean. 'You don't have to be his uncle. I only meant that there are so few people Diego warms to.' That was true. My son is very much like me in that respect.

I wanted to talk more, but Kim excused himself. 'If Diego likes,' he said as he was leaving, 'you can bring him to see me sometimes. And on those days I will try to be a good uncle.' I picked up Diego.

'*Nu, zeisele*, would you like to visit Kim sometime? Will you be a good nephew?'

He nodded his assent.

'*Meshuggeneh welt...*' I muttered to myself as I changed out of my costume. A crazy world, and how quickly and unexpectedly it had opened out to me. Those scars were markers of time; I wondered if they were also portents of change. Whatever the case, the appearance of the Korean had coincided precisely with my sense that life could not go on as it was. I took Diego home, kissed my husband on his head, smelled the dirt and sweat in his scalp, and wondered in a foregrounding of nostalgia whether he would be part of my next life. I suspected not.

I was not quite ready to relinquish him, but then fate does not operate at one's convenience. Daniel looked up from his book, embraced Diego and asked how the performance went. I gave him the brief answer the situation required, avoiding the details that would implicate us both in a stale intimacy. I put Diego to bed and my husband and I sat for a while longer, each in our chairs. Then Daniel said: 'I got a letter from my brother today. He's not coming after all. He's decided to go to Spain instead, to fight the fascists.' I sat there for the rest of the evening, consuming my own bitter tears.

The Korean's hut was some way out of the township, and even more modest than ours. It was the house his wife had died in, but you wouldn't know it, there was not a trace of a woman in there, and as I went in and was engulfed by the sadness of it all I wondered if I was only the second woman to have crossed that threshold.

As soon as we arrived Diego made his way to a small table in a corner, upon which were laid three brightly coloured books. My son had sought out the sole light and joy in the room. He picked them up one by one, fondling their pages. Kim handed one to me; they were Yiddish children's books. 'Once I used these to learn,' he said, 'but I don't need them any more.' He thought Diego might like them instead.

'My husband probably needs them even more,' I told him.

'Then give them to him.'

I regretted mentioning Daniel, and bringing him into the room with us. 'No,' I said, 'Diego will enjoy them more. Thank you.' I came closer to examine the book, so close that I brushed him, but he did not lean back into me. Perhaps his wife was also in the room with us.

Kim's home was where Diego went from then on, while I went off to rehearsals. From time to time I would return to the hut to pick Diego up and I would find Kim sleeping while my son played silently at his feet, or the two of them would be chatting away in Yiddish, or Kim would be teaching Diego Korean nursery rhymes. 'He doesn't understand the words,' he explained to me, 'he just likes the melody,' but from time to time I caught my boy using Korean words at home, for things like cups and chairs, and water. If Daniel noticed he never let on.

Our play that month was *The Cantor's Song*. The plot revolved around a young man who cannot decide whether to stay in the *shtetl* and become a cantor like his father, or to find his own way in life. Eventually he chooses his own path, and is all set for the travails that follow; however, our director had decided to rewrite the ending, so that instead of the original scenario, in which the son travels to the city to make his fortune, then, disillusioned, returns to the *shtetl* where he asks his father's forgiveness and marries his childhood sweetheart (rather than one of those city floozies), he winds up in Birobidzhan where, naturally, he finds a perfect wife who just happens to be a girl from his home town, a plain girl he had never noticed before, but now she is quite transformed, a real beauty – and they live happily ever after. As usual I didn't have an important role; this time I was just one of eleven women who sang in the background. That suited me very well – it meant I could perform without being in the spotlight or having the whole production hinge on me. If I forgot the lyrics, or even didn't turn up, it wouldn't make much of a difference. The show would go on.

It was our last rehearsal before the opening of the production that Sunday. Still flushed with song, I rode to Kim's house to pick up Diego and also to remind him about the opening night. My son was not there, however. 'I sent him home, to his father,' Kim said. He wanted to talk to me alone.

'There are some settlers I see,' he began, 'I can tell within the first week how long they will last. The ones who step out of the cattle cars in their best clothes, the women with their hair done, the men with folded kerchiefs in their breast pockets – you know they'll have a hard time. You can see it at once. The ones who arrive merely tired and poor, with no great expectations – they will stay. I have been here since the very beginning. And since then half, perhaps more, have given up and left.'

'Like my friend Anna,' I told him.

'But you haven't. Why?'

'I believe in the project,' I said. 'Don't you?'

Kim smiled. 'Sure, I believe in the project. In man, not so much.'

I didn't know what he meant.

'Now is not the best time to work on this project,' he continued. 'Better to leave it for now.'

'But it's only just begun,' I said.

'Nevertheless, sometimes fate is not on your side. I would leave now; perhaps you can come back later, when it is.'

'That's easy for you to say,' I said. 'You wouldn't understand. Once we leave we won't return.'

Kim seemed hurt. 'I'm not so very different, that's why I say it. We have a common humanity. And I feel something I have not felt since I was a boy. Something ominous. An unhappy portent. Like the feeling before you become ill, but do not really think you will. I ignored it then, and we paid dearly for it. I feel it again now. Fate is swifter than you know, and it is catching up with you. The trains come in, I hear things. I would not stay here if I were you.'

The candlelight flickered across his face, ruddy and rough, the shadow of his scar smudged in it. I reached out and cupped Kim's cheek in my palm, and he took my other hand and pressed it in his own. 'Get out,' he said. The scar gave him the authority of violence. I had escaped violence my whole life, but now I felt it was circling me, and if it was circling me then it was circling Diego too. I wondered if this was why I performed in these plays, to create the buffer of a fantastical past. And if that buffer was as flimsy as the paper screen through which the villain would inevitably burst, and because his shadow had loomed behind it for so long nobody could say they didn't see it coming. The problem is there are so many shadows, one cannot be afraid of all of them.

'What about you?' I asked, and Kim answered without hesitation.

'I have exhausted my stock of exile. I'm staying.'

It was nearly the same thing Daniel said to me the next day when I brought up the idea of leaving. 'I'm not going anywhere,' he said. 'Once is sufficient for a lifetime.' And since he was sitting in his usual chair, a pamphlet in his hands, it seemed to be a declaration that he would stay sitting in that same spot forever, whatever happened.

He did not say, '*We* are not going anywhere.' Perhaps he knew he had no power beyond himself. So I did not mention it again. I tried to let the idea rest, like something left in the dark, as if doing so would degrade it, would separate it from the essential. But it would not rest or die; the idea had a life of its own. I do not believe in man either. But I believe in fate, and in prophecy.

It is the first performance of *The Cantor's Song*. I have been singing on and off for half an hour and already my throat is sore. Since it is the opening night, Daniel is here too. He and Diego are sitting in the third row; Kim is in the second from the back. I can feel the creak of the boards beneath my feet, the heat of the bodies around me, the calluses on the hand of the woman to my right and the thrum of a production of which I feel barely a part. My voice is weak, disconnected from me somehow. I wonder if I am getting sick.

The audience registers the thunderstorm before we performers do. I have been watching them, how they glance up at the ceiling and at each other. Then the crack becomes a boom, as if a mighty fist has slammed down next to this modest building, which shudders in its wake. A small child yelps; it is Diego. We all stop still. Someone has opened the back door to look outside, and I can see flashes of pink lighting up the sky. Everyone, even the actors, is thinking that the performance outside is better than the one in here. Sensing our growing distraction, the director halts the performance mid-song and announces an interval. We all rush outside.

It is then that Kim catches me by the arm and asks me if I have made my decision. He whispers it against the flood of bodies, a small presentiment of the future in the midst of the smouldering present, and he asks it like a persistent suitor, who cannot wait even one day more for the response that will determine everything. As he speaks I can see that Daniel and Diego are trying to find me. There is a lull in the sky, an exhausted glow, and then an almighty crack rends it again. The lightning storm seems to be taking place all around us, but in a horseshoe shape, with just a narrow corridor of calm. Diego is gripping his father's hand, and when he spies me he runs over and clasps himself firmly to my legs, like wet cloth.

Daniel follows, holds his hand out for Kim to shake. 'Comrade,' he says, politely but not warmly, for he hasn't yet figured out what role this man plays in our lives. With Diego still wrapped around me, his head still buried in the drapery of my costume, I reach one hand out for Daniel's, and the other for Kim's. The fields of Birobidzhan light up and shiver, but there is no rain yet, only wind, as the whole town turns out to marvel, to be thrilled by this violence, to get swept up in it all.

Acknowledgements

This book is dedicated to my mother, Gail Jones, for reasons too numerous to mention. I am also grateful to everyone else who gave encouragement, inspiration or support while I was working on it, especially Robert Podbereski and Susan Midalia, Bert Giorgi, Noreen Jones, Drusilla Modjeska, Vic Burrows, Prue Kerr, Isabel Moutinho, Karin Derkley, Lauren Bourke, Emma Boyd, Katie Arpino, Christina Browning, Laurie Steed and Paulina Aranda-Mena. Also Terri-ann White, Lucy Dougan and David Carlin. Thank you.

ABOUT THE AUTHOR

Kyra Giorgi was born in Perth and has lived in Melbourne, Scotland, Portugal, Turkey and Germany. She has a PhD in History from La Trobe University. She now lives in Sydney.